THE SACRIFICE

DIANE MATCHECK

The Sacrifice

FARRAR STRAUS GIROUX

NEW YORK

Library of Congress Cataloging-in-Publication Data
Matcheck, Diane.
The sacrifice / Diane Matcheck. — 1st ed.
   p. cm.
Summary: When her father's death leaves her orphaned and an outcast among her
Apsaalooka (Crow) people, a fifteen-year-old sets out to avenge his death and prove that
she, not her dead twin brother, is destined to be the Great One.
   ISBN 0-374-36378-1
   1. Crow Indians—Juvenile fiction. [1. Crow Indians—Fiction. 2. Indians of
North America—Fiction. 3. Orphans—Fiction. 4. Self-perception—Fiction.] I. Title.
PZ7.M423967Sag 1998
[Fic]—dc21   97-36408

To my mother and father,
who raised me to believe in dreams

For what is a man profited,
if he shall gain the whole world,
and lose his own soul?
or what shall a man give in exchange for his soul?

—MATTHEW 16:26

THE SACRIFICE

1

THE GIRL CLAWED THE WIND-WHIPPED HAIR OUT of her eyes with bloody hands, and listened.

She had heard a foreign voice, but the sound was difficult to find again over the wind. She leaned forward on one knee and scanned the wide, flat valley and the gentle mountains that encircled it, searching for sign of an enemy.

The setting sun was painting the sky a brilliant orange, streaked with violet clouds. Such colors made her feel like singing. Usually, if no one was looking, she would sit back for a moment and allow herself this one pleasure. But now she kept her eyes on the ground.

The sun had dipped behind the peaks, leaving their valley dim, and her eyesight was not as sharp as that of some in her village. Still, she had learned to discern distant things by their motion. She could tell a buffalo or a deer or a horse or a pronghorn by the way the animal moved. People were easy to identify; they did not lift their heads when they sensed danger, but turned them. They ran more slowly than other large animals, and they looked as if they had legs running on top of their bodies, too, because of the pumping of their arms. When they did not want to be discovered, people walked carefully, like long-legged birds.

There was nothing to be seen in the valley now but the brown river and occasional patches of snow. The ice was just beginning to go out of the rivers, and the wind was cold and relentless across the open valley, but the girl bore discomfort easily.

Reluctantly she turned her eyes back to the buffalo carcass. If only she had heard an enemy raiding party. She would give anything for a chance to prove herself as a warrior.

She shifted to her other knee and pushed her hair back again. It snarled in a grimy black nest down her back. She was a starved-looking, long-limbed girl of fifteen winters, with eyes that smoldered from deep within, like a wildcat's eyes at night from within its den. The high cheekbones and fine, straight nose so common among her Apsaalooka people would have been beautiful on another girl, but her face was a hard mask, with a taut, thin line for a mouth. She wore crudely sewn boy's clothing: a plain buckskin shirt and leggings, gray with dirt from long wear, and a breechcloth that was now soaked with blood.

She wiped her hands on the breechcloth again, trying to stop their trembling. It gave her a dizzying sense of power to have risked joining the buffalo hunt—she still could feel the pounding of deadly hooves all around her. She did not even care that her father would be angry. Surely three buffalo felled by her hand proved she was ready for battle; how could he tell her again that she was not?

She should have defied him long ago, for then the day she had dreamed of might already have arrived. It was a day she had imagined for so many winters that the very thought of it was nearly real.

She would return to the village just after the sun had set, when the sky was green-blue. She could almost feel the charcoal that blackened her face in the sign of victory, and smell the smoke drifting from the tepees. The dogs would begin barking as she approached, and the villagers would scramble from their lodges, shouting. One and all would stare in awe at her fine war shirt, at the pretty-faced white mare she would be riding, and at the scalps snaking in the wind from her coup lance. With all eyes upon her she would thrust the lance overhead and shout, "I am the Great One!"

Then the people would rush around her to touch her finery, and beg her forgiveness—especially her friend Grasshopper—and her father would come running, to pull her from her horse and throw his arms around her. The singers would make praise songs about her, and all the people who now looked past her as though she were not there, or called her bad in the head, would beg her to feast with them and tell the story of her adventure.

At last she would be someone—the Great One—with a real name, instead of Weak-one-who-does-not-last. She would take a mighty name, reflecting her mighty deeds.

Not a single sun set without her imagining that day and that name. Of course, the real name, the right name, would not present itself until she had earned it. When that came to pass, she felt, her brother Born-great's curse would be broken.

She smiled grimly. Born-great had thought that tearing away her friend would defeat her, but he was wrong. It only made the desire in her burn stronger. She thrust her stone blade into the buffalo's chest with a vengeance.

"It is not over yet," she told her brother's ghost. Her big dirty-gold gelding, grazing a few paces away, snorted and ambled toward her. "I was not talking to you, Bull," she said, patting his broad, black face and evading his attempts to nip her. Bull was a homely beast with a lazy gait and a habit of biting, and he was too big to mount without a step up. But he was solid, and the only creature she trusted.

She buried her knife in the carcass again, pretending not to hear her father shouting at her through the wind as he came striding across the dead grass.

"I asked you a question," Chews-the-bear said. His talk was stubby-sounding and full of whistles, because all but one of his front teeth were snapped off jagged or gone completely.

"We needed the meat, and the hides," she said, continuing to gut the carcass as though nothing were wrong.

"You know only hunters are permitted on buffalo hunts." The wrinkles carved into his brown face made his scowl seem even more severe. "You might have stampeded the herd. Then the tribal guard would have *your* hide!"

She tensed at the mention of a whipping from the guard—one man had never recovered from it. But she *was* a hunter, a good hunter, and would never have startled the herd. Her father knew this, too; that was not his real fear.

"But," she said, "I did not stampede the herd. I brought down three buffalo."

Chews-the-bear worked his tongue around the stumps of his front teeth, gathering his thoughts, as he always did when angry. "Did you thank that animal for giving up its life?"

"Yes," she lied, wrenching the intestines free and heaving them onto the billowing grass. She had no intention of thanking any animal she killed. It was *she* who had killed it, with her sweat and her skill. She picked up the knife again.

Chews-the-bear seized her wrist, and she dropped the knife in surprise and pain. "Have some respect," he hissed, "and stop hacking at the beast."

He threw her hand down. She rubbed her wrist, seething.

"A true warrior hates to kill," said Chews-the-bear. "Not so you. Sometimes you make my skin cold."

Sometimes she made her own skin cold, too, the girl realized with alarm, but suddenly she heard a sound that pressed the thought down.

She held up her hand in warning. "Voices."

Chews-the-bear squinted, listening. A strand of greasy gray hair caught on his lips. He heard only the wind humming through the matted buffalo grass, but this did not mean his daughter had not heard something.

Presently Chews-the-bear broke the silence. "You hear one of the boys. A group of them ran off into the hills earlier."

She wished he had not reminded her of them. A tight feeling gripped her chest.

Chews-the-bear narrowed his eyes. "You disobeyed me because Grasshopper has joined with Laughing Crow and his friends, and you are jealous, is it not true?"

She felt slapped in the face. She and Grasshopper had become friends because both were outsiders, but now that Grasshopper had become a Crazy-dog-wishing-to-die, even Laughing Crow looked up to him, and he had no more use for a crazy girl with a crazy father. Her chest tightened further as she remembered last night's humiliation. She had walked past Laughing Crow and his friends, and they began mocking and insulting her, as always. But this time Grasshopper was with them, and just to better the others, he had called her an orphan—the vilest insult in the Apsaalooka tongue. To be called an orphan was to be called less than a dog.

"Grasshopper is not worth your jealousy," Chews-the-bear said as though he were spitting out something sickening. It enraged her, although only hours ago she had found comfort in the same thought.

"He is my only friend," she burst out. Then she added, "Except for you."

Chews-the-bear widened his stance against the wind. "I am not your friend," he said. "I am your father."

He gave her chin a tap upward and she jerked away. "You must remember who you are, daughter. You are destined to be one of the greatest Apsaalooka ever to live. A boy like Grasshopper is beneath you."

I would not be so certain, she dared not say. "My stomach is sick with being whispered about and laughed at. Why do you not let me show them that I can ride and shoot as well as any of them?"

"There is no room in a warrior's heart for vanity."

Maddened, she leaped to her feet and began pacing. She was certain the village would accept her as a warrior—it was not unheard of for a woman—if only she could show them. But since Born-great's death, Chews-the-bear had been afraid. "How can I be the Great One if I am permitted to do nothing?" she demanded.

"One day when you are ready . . ."

How many times she had heard that! She snatched up the bloody knife and thrust it toward him. "I *am* ready. This"—she kicked the dead buffalo, and her father flinched—"is 'ready.' Not just to hunt, but to make war."

"You are *too* ready," Chews-the-bear said, chopping the air with a leathery hand. "You are reckless, dangerous."

"I will never be ready enough for you!"

"Do you want to get yourself killed?" he shouted. The question struck them both like a blow.

"You are afraid," she said, unable to stop herself. "You are afraid I will be killed like Born-great!"

Chews-the-bear shut his eyes, and his craggy face stiffened with pain—not physical pain, but the other kind. She took a certain satisfaction in having hurt her father. She knew he was listening again to the scream from long ago.

Her twin brother had been four winters old when he rode on the raid against the Cheyenne. No one intended that he get into the fighting; he had been taken only for his medicine. The whole village believed that Born-great had powerful medicine, because an owl had foretold it to Chews-the-bear in a dream: his wife would die bearing twins, and one of the twins would die young, but the other would become one of the greatest Apsaalooka ever to live. Not only was Born-great thought to be the Great One, he also wore an owl-shaped *bacoritsitse*—sacred stone—around his neck. Wherever he went, he brought good fortune—good hunting, good weather, good water. They had no reason to doubt that his medicine would be strong against the Cheyenne.

It had taken three men to hold Chews-the-bear from running back into the Cheyenne ambush when he heard his son screaming for him. Those three men saved Chews-the-bear's life. That made four survivors. The village called that winter the winter the Cheyenne killed eleven men.

For a time Chews-the-bear had insisted that Born-great still lived, and tried to mount a rescue party, but the people no longer believed his dream, they could not forgive, and they could see he had lost his mind along with his son. No one ever followed him into battle again.

After a time he gave up the dream that his son was alive. Many days he did not rise from bed, and when he did he seemed to be sleepwalking. He went on this way for many moons, looking right through his daughter, until the afternoon she convinced him that he had made a mistake, that she was the Great One.

Although the scream still haunted him, eleven winters after the ambush, Chews-the-bear thought that Born-great's death was as the dream had foretold. He did not know that the scream haunted the girl, too, although she had not been present to hear it. He did not know that it was not the Cheyenne, but she, who had caused Born-great's death.

After a time, with immense control, he said only, "It is disrespectful to speak of the dead."

The girl felt sick with a sudden fear that she was nothing but evil. "Perhaps there was a mistake," she blurted. "Perhaps I really am the Weak-one-who-does-not-last, and I should have been the one to die."

She turned away, but Chews-the-bear grasped her wrist.

"It is I who made the mistake," he said, "in thinking that your brother was the one because it is not usual for females to become warriors. It is also not usual, when twins are born, for both to survive. Usually one is weak and soon dies. The people call you Weak-one because no one expected you to live. But you are not usual. And when you are ready, then the people will be ready for you. Then you will make a name for yourself. Your name is not Weak-one. Never let me hear you speak it again."

"You don't understand," she said.

"I understand more than you think I do."

Just as a panic struck her that he knew what she had done to her brother, that he had found the broken medicine, an urgent noise snatched her attention. Head cocked, she stood alert, trying to catch a thread of sound through the wind.

"War cries," she whispered.

This time Chews-the-bear heard, too.

2

IN THE DUSK, SHE MADE OUT A SWARM OF DARK figures pouring down a steep, stony slide on a nearby mountain, and spilling out onto the plain toward the village.

They were definitely people, on horseback.

"They are not headed toward the horses," Chews-the-bear said. He ran the few paces to Bull and jerked the gelding's head from the grass. "Help me up," he commanded. His daughter ran to him and shoved his foot up. He swung onto the horse's back. "Lie down and hide. Do not move, no matter what happens." He gave a kick, and Bull bolted toward the village.

The girl flattened herself into the grass, her cheekbone pressed against something sharp. She was unable to see a thing but her bloodstained, broken fingernails and the tangle of grass in her face.

The distant thudding and cries of the beginning clash

carried to her on the wind. Her bow and quiver were strapped to Bull's back, and she cursed herself for being caught without them. No one could stop her from fighting in the midst of an attack. And after the battle, how could Chews-the-bear argue against slain enemies? She might stand before the council fire she had been dreaming of all her life, if only she had a bow.

She raised her head. Although the village had been attacked many times, she had always been off by herself in the hills, or shoved into a lodgeful of women and children where she could see nothing.

Slowly, on her elbows and toes, she crawled toward the foothills that flanked one side of the village. She reached their cover of scrub pine and juniper and scrambled up to run toward the fighting.

Twenty-five or thirty warriors on horseback struggled forward among the Apsaalooka, slashing with knives and swinging studded clubs. She knew from the leader's blue-and-yellow shirt that the invaders were Headcutters. Amid the war cries and howls of agony, she felt herself unexpectedly pierced by fear.

The reputation of the Headcutters, or Lakota, as they called themselves, was well known to her. Her people were frequently attacked, often for their horses, for Apsaalooka horses were coveted by many, but although many tribes took prisoners of women and children to adopt into their own families, Headcutters were as likely to kill as to kidnap. She crushed her fear down harshly, as she would cuff a begging dog, and cursed again under her breath at being without a weapon.

Her eyes searched for Chews-the-bear but did not find him. She spotted Grasshopper's father, Broken Branch, trying to pull an attacker from his horse. Unable to unseat the warrior, Broken Branch stabbed at his mount. As the animal's legs buckled, he leaped on the Headcutter and together they rolled under the falling horse.

The girl circled wide around the village on the hillside, watching for her father. From up here, the warriors seemed melted together into a single living, raging thing. As she drew closer to the other side of the village, she could see from the riderless horses plunging about that several Headcutters had fallen. Some were already fleeing along the river.

She saw a flash of white—Chews-the-bear's doeskin leggings. They disappeared into the swarm again. She reached the plain, slid into the grass, and began creeping along the edge of camp. Occasionally she tipped her head up to see where she was. Through the haze of grass she could make out her father grappling with the blue-and-yellow-shirted warrior as he tried to run up the hillside. The Headcutter leader had lost his horse, and they were struggling hand to hand over Chews-the-bear's lance.

Suddenly Chews-the-bear twisted his lance free and lunged into the enemy. Then he stepped backward. A blot of bright red splattered the Headcutter leader's war shirt.

But the blood was not his own. Chews-the-bear took another step back, and another, then crashed to his knees. Blood ran from his rib cage.

The Headcutter caught Chews-the-bear by the hair before he could collapse to the ground. With his blade the warrior sliced down along the old man's head and began peeling back the scalp. A groan forced its way through the gaps in Chews-the-bear's clenched teeth.

"No!" his daughter screamed and flew up from the grass, hurling herself at the Headcutter. "No! No!" She shrieked and pounded and clawed his blood-soaked chest, and, finding his face, dug her fingers into his eyes. Then a crack of lightning flashed through her and she was sliding to the ground. The thudding and cries and horses' bellowing grew distant, and as she sighed into darkness a thought, strangely, brought her peace: her twin brother had finally exacted the perfect revenge.

3

BORN-GREAT, CHUBBY EVEN AT FOUR WINTERS old, stood in the doorway of their lodge, grinning. He had a quirky, disarming smile that opened many hearts to him, but not his sister's. The broken black owl hanging against his bare chest seemed to point at her with its remaining wing.

"You thought you killed me," Born-great said in a voice that seemed too old for him.

She froze in her bed of buffalo robes, as though by not moving she would not be seen. "You are dead," she rasped.

"But I did not die," he said.

She cleared her throat. "You are dead."

"I am your twin. I am a part of you," he said, still smiling.

Born-great opened his arms and began walking toward her. She screamed, scrambling backward, against the sloping wall of the tepee. "I killed you!"

17

"No," Born-great said, and kept coming. "You killed yourself."

Stars began raining in her head. The wind swelled, lifting her from her dream. She was sweating, clenched in a ball on her bed robes. The light was dim, and her panting was like smoke in the cold air as her eyes darted around the lodge. She was used to the nightmares, but still it took time to be certain her brother was truly not there.

She was alone. The wind beat against the tepee, rushing in around the door flap, carrying the sound of a woman wailing.

The girl pushed her covers aside and sat up. She waited for the pounding in her head to subside, fingering the crusted wound on her crown.

It had been two days since her father's death. The burial could be delayed no longer. She must see that he was prepared for his journey to the Beyond-country. It would be a difficult journey this time. Many winters ago, when he had been mauled by the she-grizzly, Chews-the-bear's spirit-soul had journeyed to the Beyond-country and back again, but he was a young warrior then and traveled in a time of plenty, When-the-leaves-turn-yellow. Now he was old and tired, and the season was spring, when mountains and rivers make dangerous crossing, and food is scarce.

She did not eat or bathe, but went straight to her task. She packed two parfleches to bulging with pine nuts and dried berries, and another of the flat, folded rawhide boxes with pemmican.

The tepee creaked under the force of the wind as she gathered her father's belongings. Stuffed deep in his quiver she found the wolf-tail moccasins he should be buried in. She laid them with everything else on the old, worn bearskin robe, and, bundling it into her arms, she stepped out into the flat gray day. At her feet lay the body of her father, wrapped in part of their tepee cover.

As she knelt down, she noticed an unfamiliar parfleche, painted with yellow diamonds, jutting out from her father's shroud. With a dry mouth, she slid the parfleche out, untied its thongs, and opened the rawhide flaps. It was filled with strips of *barutskitue,* the dried chokecherry mash that her father prized.

She looked around. A few young children and dogs shuffled by. She saw none of the boys from Laughing Crow's group. They were probably inside, shivering under their covers, drinking their mothers' licorice-root tea, she thought scornfully. Cut-ear's two wives stood outside their lodge restaking the windbreak. One of the women had cropped her hair in mourning for a brother. She glanced over, and the girl hurriedly looked down.

The mysterious gift made her uneasy. It was not the first; there had been many given to her, in the days before she had convinced her father that she was the Great One. It was a time she remembered only vaguely. Night and day the people came to look at Born-great, and in the excitement, his twin was not much noticed. Those first years, there was a grandmother who took care of her, but after the grandmother's death, the girl ran wild, fighting the camp dogs for scraps. It was then that the mysterious gifts began, always left while she slept. Food, sometimes clothing. After she stole one of Born-great's many toy bows and taught herself to shoot, she once awoke to a gift of arrows. Now it struck her that through all these winters, deep in her heart she had felt the gifts had been left by her father.

She breathed deeply. How could she have thought such a thing? Her father had seen only Born-great, hardly knew she was alive, until long after her brother was dead. Angrily she grabbed Chews-the-bear's moccasins to slip them on his feet, so she could be finished with her task.

Last night she had dressed his body in ceremonial clothes: his ermine-striped shirt and horsehair-fringed leggings, his bone-pipe breastplate, the old blue-and-buff-beaded gauntlets her mother had sewn for him when pregnant with her and Born-great. The moccasins were of soft elk skin, a wolf's tail knotted to each heel signifying that he had counted coup—touched an enemy in battle—a higher-ranked war exploit than killing an enemy. Chews-the-bear had worn these moccasins at council and on war parties long ago, before the Cheyenne slaughter, when he was still a respected man.

A different pair of moccasins, blood-brown, stepped into the edge of her vision, a wide, red sash dragging on the frosty ground beside them. She knew they belonged to Grasshopper, but she ignored him.

They had been friends, before, drawn together by their similar lack of status. One of Grasshopper's legs was shorter than the other, and his left arm was small and bent. He could not even pull a bow. There could be no stolen horses or scalps or weapons snatched in battle for him.

He might have led a tolerable life as a medicine man like his father, but to Grasshopper such a life was no life. He wanted to be nothing less than a warrior.

Yet the only brave thing a crippled boy could do in battle was die.

So, a few moons ago, Grasshopper had become a Crazy-dog-wishing-to-die. He was by far the youngest member of the brotherhood; usually only old men who were tired of living, or perhaps someone who had suffered losses so great he could not bear to go on, became Crazy-dogs. Grasshopper was only fourteen winters old. He looked gallant with the brotherhood's long red sash trailing from his waist, and was good at talking the crosswise way of the Crazy-dogs—saying the opposite of what he meant. He had become wildly popular among the other boys, boasting in crosswise talk that the next chance he got he would stake his sash to the ground before the advancing enemy and die unflinchingly. Some of the girls even began to look at him—a cripple!—with soft eyes.

She had stayed in the shadows, forgotten and nearly mad with envy. But it was Grasshopper's betrayal that she could not forgive, his calling her an orphan.

"I am not sorry for what I said about you," Grasshopper said in a cracked voice. Although she was used to his crosswise talk, she had difficulty translating now. "I am glad that your father is dead. My father says that you must live the wretched life of an orphan, that you are not welcome as a daughter in his lodge."

She flinched at the word *orphan.*

"*Di axparaaxe,*" she said coldly. It was not as harsh an insult as his calling her an orphan a few nights ago, but she said it with a finality that he could not fail to understand. She was not just insulting him, she was telling him that from now on, he *was* a ghost. He was dead to her, and she would never speak to him again.

One of the blood-brown moccasins scuffed at a stone. She forced herself to unwrap the stiff yellow shroud. Without touching her father's feet, her hands slid the wolf-tail moccasins on. She could hardly see through her black hair streaming across her face, but she did not stop.

Grasshopper spoke again. "You are strong enough to bury Chews-the-bear yourself. I will not help."

She continued to look through her hair at the moccasins she was tying.

"Please—my heart is light with joy because of what I did. Won't you . . ." He did not finish his sentence; perhaps it was too difficult to express crosswise. Her fingers faltered with the laces.

"I would be ashamed to be your brother," Grasshopper said quietly.

She pulled hard on the knot and her hand slipped against her father's ankle. The dead cold shot through her arm like a pain. She flung the shroud over the feet and jumped up. She had not finished tying the second wolf-tail moccasin, but she did not care. Let him tie it himself. As fast as she could without running, she hurried away across the grass, toward the river. No sound rose above the wind from behind her.

The horses stood waiting with sharpened ears. Bull greeted her with his usual snort.

"I have some work for you, Bull," she said, dodging his teeth as she slipped a halter over his big face. "Today I bury my father. I need you to carry his body and his burial things up to the ridge where we once sat to smoke and watch the sun set." A tightness pulled at her throat, and she said no more.

The digging was slow. The dirt was almost as hard as the buffalo-shoulder-blade tool she hacked at it with. She piled the larger rocks to the side to cover the grave later. When she stood not quite to her knees in the trench she hit frozen ground. She turned to widening the pit. Finally, sweaty and light-headed, she swung the digging tool away.

With his head toward the sunset, the girl laid her father in the grave. She covered the dull yellow shroud with a new buffalo robe, for the air was cold and the sky was surely not yet empty of snow. Then one by one she placed beside Chews-the-bear's body the other things he would need on his journey.

The *barutskitue,* fresh and dried buffalo meat, the berries and pine nuts. Three new pairs of moccasins. His pipe and tobacco. His finely carved elk-antler bow, which had leaned against a backrest for several winters now. Its sheath of rattlesnake skin crinkled like a brown leaf in her hand.

She picked up his lance, and saw again the image of her father struggling with the Headcutter.

Resting on one knee for a moment, she balanced the spear in her hands. It was a joy to hold, but it had seen little blood since Chews-the-bear wrested it from a Blackfoot in battle many winters ago. Her father had not wanted to break the gleaming head, which was as long as her forearm and knapped of black obsidian, the mysterious, rocklike substance that shone like black water and cut sharper than flint. She liked to imagine that this spearhead had been cut from the black cliff in the Land of Boiling Waters. It was at that cliff that he had found Born-great's sacred stone: a thick shaving of obsidian in the shape of an owl in flight. It had fallen from the cliff to land at Chews-the-bear's feet, just as the owl in his dream had foretold.

Though there was no sun, the spearhead glinted, as though it held light of its own. She had seen other colors of obsidian—milky green and red-brown mingled with black—but the color that enthralled her was pure black. It was utter black in its depths and faded to clear at its edges. It was like a living thing, black fire, power: the sharpest substance known. But very brittle.

Reluctantly she laid the lance in her father's grave. Her knee cracked as she stood up and drew her flint knife.

Bull was grazing so close behind her that even over the wind she could hear the grinding of his teeth. She pressed his head against her chest and began sawing through his coarse black mane, and when she had finished, she cropped his tail. She stuffed the hairs under her father's robe where they would not be blown away. Some mourners killed and buried a man's horses, but she had several practical considerations. She could not bury four horses without a great deal of help, and she would not ask any. This way, since each hair would become a fine horse in the Beyond-country, her father would own many horses instead of only four, making him a wealthy and respected man again. And though she would be expected to give the other three animals away, she could keep Bull for her own.

She was glad of these practical considerations, because one creature she could never have killed was a horse. Especially not Bull.

She lifted up the hide of the grizzly her father had long ago battled. The men who had distracted the bear from him and driven a spear through it had given him the hide, because he had earned it with his courage. The skin side had been painted with figures showing his many exploits, and as the robe billowed in the wind the faded horses galloped across it. The fur had thinned over the years. It was especially bare at her father's teethmarks, where so many fingers had admired it that it was worn right through. When she was a child, her own slender fingertips had rubbed the ragged little flap to a dark polish. One last time she slid a finger through. Her father had been mauled by a grizzly bear and had bitten back! How many times she had listened to him tell the story, secretly wishing something like this would happen to her, while he tried to make it a lesson as dry as clay dust.

She spread the grizzly hide over the grave and began piling rocks on it. She worked hastily, not caring when her fingertips were caught between the stones. She was sweating and breathing hard as she heaved the last one into place.

The frigid wind chilled her inside the sweat-dampened skin shirt as she pushed up the sleeves and drew her knife again. She knew without thinking that she would not cut off her hair, as many mourners did in spite of the humiliation, nor would she cut off a finger joint. Rather, she rested the sharp edge on her bare forearm and, holding her breath, dragged the blade across.

Then she cut her other arm, and her legs. She felt no pain, only the sensation of blood flowing down her limbs. She reached out her arms over the grave and watched her blood, sprayed by the wind, splatter onto the rocks. It gave her a feeling of relief, as if something bad were going out of her.

"You are gone, do not turn back," she said. "We wish to fare well." That was all the ceremony she knew. She should cry now. But she never cried. There were no tears in her.

Before Born-great's death, Chews-the-bear had been a chief and a respected man. The whole village should be here mourning his death. He had earned a burial plat-form flocked with red streamers, and a long procession led by drummers. Yet here he lay in a shallow trough, at-tended by no one but an orphan girl.

Orphan.

She was back where she had started: no one, nothing, dependent on charity and her own wits. The humiliation was unbearable. She could not think of adoption. She was fifteen winters old—she should have been married by now! And adoption would mean crawling on her belly to Grasshopper and his family or to one of the others who had spurned her and her father.

In legend, orphans begged the gods to have pity, and with their help became great warriors and returned home in glory. But what god would favor a murderer? Indeed, Born-great would try to destroy her at every turn. But she had managed this far on her own. She could do it. She must do it.

It is not over yet, she told Born-great silently.

"Father, your spirit is still near. Hear me," she said into the wind. "The owl said that one of your children would die young and one would number among the greatest Apsaalooka ever to live."

She looked at her arms and legs. The wind had dried the blood to a sticky, dusty film. "My legs are swift, and my arms strong. You have taught me the ways of a warrior, but I am never allowed to fight. I am tired of running races against no one and shooting with no reward.

"The time has come for me to prove myself, Father." She paused, wiping the blowing hair out of her face and gathering her courage as the idea took shape in her mouth. "Your death must be avenged. Therefore I will go with the revenge party and I will kill a Headcutter.

"Yes, I will kill a Headcutter," she repeated to herself as if the words tasted good.

She turned to Bull and clambered up the travois onto his back. "They must let me go, Bull," she said into his ear. "I am his kin."

4

THE COUNCIL FIRE HISSED AND SPAT BLUE FLAMES.
Sobs for lost sons and husbands rose with the sparks into
the night, where clouds slid past the sliver of moon. Most
of the villagers were already seated, and the elders and
warriors with painted faces and bodies gathered like vari-
colored moths around the fire.

Laughing Crow, dark and fierce-looking, was walking
toward the war party, and a group of boys eddied around
him. Everyone wanted to be Laughing Crow's friend because no one wanted to be his enemy. He was big for his
age and an excellent archer, and he was as deadly with
words as he was with arrows. The girl noticed Grasshopper was not with him. She scanned the gathering and
saw her old friend sitting next to his mother and her kin.
His father, Broken Branch, was an important medicine
man and stood near the fire with the other council members. He looked unusually young for a man of forty or

forty-five winters, with a dignified bearing and eyes that seemed to see more than others'. Tonight those eyes followed his oldest son, Lies-down-in-water, who would be riding with the revenge party.

She had painted a yellow stripe across the bridge of her nose and her cheekbones, and wore a freshly sewn buffalo-skin shirt, leggings, and moccasins. Beneath her shirt she wore a medicine necklace made from the owl's wing. It felt like a spark swinging against her skin.

How that owl had tantalized her, hanging from Born-great's throat. In her child's mind it was the difference between them, the mysterious power with which her brother attracted all the toys and treats and reverent touches. The day they were preparing to set off against the Cheyenne, when the fawning over Born-great was unbearable, she broke it. When all his protectors had for once wandered a few steps out of sight, she dashed at him and worked her thin fingers around the owl and pinched with all her might, until a delicious crack shot from it as she snapped a wing off. It was mostly the sound that she remembered. And she knew the memory was real, because hidden away for eleven winters she had kept the broken wing.

That night they left on their raid against the Cheyenne, and two nights later Born-great was trampled in the ambush. But that was not the end of him. His ghost cast a long, vengeful shadow.

Now, however, she would finally have her chance. The things she would need for the war party stood packed and waiting inside her lodge, ready to be snatched up and strapped onto Bull's back. She walked to the outer edge of the crowd, where the firelight did not reach, and knelt in the darkness.

Redwing, a tall man of seventy winters and the leader of the village, lifted his hands to quiet the crowd. "It is time," he said.

As the people took their places, Redwing, Broken Branch, and the other elders sat in a half circle facing them. A splendid pipe, with a red bowl shaped like a horsehead and snakes carved around the stem, was lit, raised to the four sacred directions, and passed quietly among the elders. The men did not speak, but each sent his silent prayer for victory with the smoke up to the spirits. The fire licked around the logs and popped in the cold night air.

She was hungry like the fire, but she had to wait until the right moment to speak. When the smoking ended, there would be women calling for someone to avenge the murders of their family members, and songs of war from the scouts. The Crazy-dogs-wishing-to-die would vow to run into the middle of the Headcutter camp and stake their red sashes to the ground with their lances and call out, "It is a good day to die," and fight to the death. Finally, Cut-ear, the leader of the party, would announce his men. Then she would speak.

But all these preliminaries passed so quickly she felt rushed ahead of her courage.

Cut-ear was stepping forward. "I have heard the cries

of my wife's mother for her son," he said angrily. "She has handed me the war pipe, and I shall carry it. I carry it for all you who cry."

He motioned another man forward. "Moose's Beard will be my scout," he announced. Moose's Beard wore a wolfskin tied onto his back, denoting his role.

It was almost time. Cut-ear introduced his herald and two more scouts. As soon as he finished speaking, there would be a beat of silence, and she must act.

"And also, on his first raid," Cut-ear said as the men crowded behind him, "I take Laughing Crow."

She choked back a shout of indignation as Laughing Crow strode forward and stood with the warriors. Her cheeks burned at being forced to share the warpath and glory with this worm, but she had no time for anger. Now was the moment.

She stood. "I, too," she began in a whisper, and had to clear her throat. "I, too, wish to go with the war party," she said.

For an instant it seemed no one had heard. Then some of the people turned and looked at her. She almost wished she could hide her face paint and new clothes. There was a silence, then a murmuring. She forced herself onward.

"A Headcutter killed my father," she said, louder. "As my father's kin I have the right to settle this matter by slaying a Headcutter."

"Let us have no foolishness," Redwing said flatly.

"You have no such right," said Not-turning-around. "And no right to speak at council."

Cut-ear stood ready to continue, ignoring the interruption.

"I am well trained and ready for battle," the girl said. "I felled three buffalo during the last hunt."

"That is nothing to boast of," Cut-ear snapped. "Be grateful the tribal guard did not whip you until you could never ride again."

Moose's Beard looked at the girl appraisingly. "She does have a fire," he said. Then to her he added, "But hunting is not war. One of your father's other relations will avenge his death."

Redwing spoke. "Other women mourn, but they do not go on the warpath. Why do you not do as they do? Ask one of the warriors to avenge your father's death for you."

"Perhaps she cannot pay; her father was not well off," a woman's voice said.

The girl gritted her teeth. "I don't need a warrior—I *am* a warrior."

"Don't worry, little one, I will kill a Headcutter for you," Laughing Crow called to her.

"That is enough," Broken Branch said.

The girl thrust a finger toward Laughing Crow. "He is only two winters older than I."

"At your age," Moose's Beard said, lifting his chin in her direction, "two winters is a long time. Two winters can be the difference between boy and man."

"And she's not even a boy," Laughing Crow said under his breath.

"I am more of a man than you'll ever be," she spat.

"I am wondering if that is not true." Broken Branch looked coldly at Laughing Crow.

The murmuring had grown loud. She knew it was going against her, but there was no backing down.

"Weak-one," Broken Branch said, "have no fear, your father's death will be avenged by the war party."

"Let us continue," said Not-turning-around. The girl could feel her moment sliding away.

"I will be recognized," she insisted.

Broken Branch stood, walked a pace or two, and dropped his head back as if to look for guidance in the stars. His loose black hair fell nearly to his knees. "Your father was a courageous man and my lifelong friend." He stretched an arm out toward Lies-down-in-water. "I give you my word, my son will avenge your father's death." Lies-down-in-water, eyes fixed on hers, nodded once. A strange, hot embarrassment pierced her.

Before she could think, Broken Branch addressed the crowd. "I say it here before the entire village, that all may know I am sincere: This girl is welcome in my lodge. I will gladly adopt her as my own daughter."

Then he said gently, "But we cannot permit you to go to war."

She felt ashamed by Broken Branch's kindness, drawn to him, and frightened by her sudden softening. She knew what the people were thinking: she must be adopted, even at her age, because no man wanted her.

"But you let my brother go to war when he was four winters old."

"That was a mistake," said Broken Branch heavily.

"Because I am the one," she said. "My brother died because I am the Great One!" In her heart she had never been convinced that this was true, but she clung to it.

"This kind of nonsense is what killed the other one," bellowed Redwing, "and many good men with him."

Murmurs and comments tumbled in her ears.

"She is bad in the head, like her father . . ."

"I was against it then and I am against it now."

"You must let me go," she cried.

"I have nothing to say." A young voice slipped through the clamor. Grasshopper, his sash trailing on the ground, made his way toward the council fire. "I have nothing to say."

"Enough," said an elder who had been silent. "This is an Apsaalooka council."

Broken Branch said, "I would hear my son speak."

Over muffled complaints, Grasshopper faced the people. With his back to the fire, his expression was shrouded in darkness.

"I do not know this girl better than anyone else here," he said crosswise. She tried to block him out, but the unexpected strength in his voice rang in her ears. "And she

35

is a worse warrior than Laughing Crow. She should not be permitted to go."

The crowd drowned his voice, or perhaps she stopped hearing for a moment. She could scarcely believe that Grasshopper had spoken on her behalf. She was filled with an irrational fear.

"The discussion is ended," Redwing said.

"Let us be off," said Cut-ear, and the warriors called for their wives and sisters to bring the horses.

The villagers began crowding around the men, wishing them well.

"I am not bad in the head," she cried.

Some of the villagers looked in her direction, then turned away.

"You are right," Broken Branch said quietly beside her. She turned in surprise. "You are not bad in the head. You are bad in the heart. I know you have good reason to have a bad heart, Weak One, but what is the reason to keep a bad heart?"

To the medicine man's question she had no answer. Could those eyes of his see that she was a murderer? "I am not the Weak One," she lashed out.

"I know," he said.

The warriors were packed and mounted and turning upriver, while the people trotted alongside urging them on. They passed her by as though she did not exist.

"One day I will arrive in this village with a black face," she shouted at them bitterly. "And you people who laugh at me tonight will beg me to dine in your lodges, and sing praise songs about me. Your children will sing songs about me. And your children's children."

Broken Branch touched her elbow, and she jerked away. He said gently, "My lodge will be open to you, when you are ready."

She was so ashamed all she could do was run.

Laughing Crow raced up on horseback and cut her off, wheeling his mare around so closely in front of her that the animal stepped on her foot. She clenched her jaw, refusing to let him see her pain. She slapped the animal's flank, but Laughing Crow held it firm. He said nothing, only sneered at her for an instant, then whipped his mare soundly, and with a lurch he was gone.

The girl ran back to her lodge and collapsed onto her bed robes. Rolling onto her back, she looked up through the open smoke flaps into the black, starless sky, and suddenly she knew what to do. She had nothing to lose. She would follow the war party. She would carefully keep her distance so that she would not be discovered, and show herself when they had gone too far to send her back. Boys sometimes tried this tactic, and sometimes it worked.

No, Born-great would not stop her this way.

The girl waited until she heard no more voices or shufflings, until she could be certain that no one was still afoot in the village. Then, when she could stand the wait no longer, she rose and gathered her gear and listened at the lodge entrance. All was quiet. In the cold air her breath frosted as she made her way through the sleeping village, trying not to disturb the dogs. They knew her well and let her pass unchallenged.

The horses shifted uneasily at being approached in the middle of the night.

"Wake up, Bull," she whispered, patting the big horse's neck. "We are traveling tonight after all."

5

SHE LOOKED OUT OVER THE DARK TANGLE OF
rivers that snaked in their separate directions toward the
surrounding mountains, and breathed in the cold wind
deeply so the damp, earthy smell of spring would waken
her senses. She had grown sleepy from riding so long.

"We are away from home now, Bull," she whispered.
The girl had never traveled much beyond Where-the-
rivers-come-together, the place where three rivers joined
to form Big River before it spilled into their valley. From
here she must be especially watchful, for enemies and
for the war party's trail. The war party would ride along
the near river for a while, then turn toward the sunrise
and the open plains. She would follow the river, too, and
when it grew light she would begin searching for signs.
She pressed her heels into Bull's ribs.

The wind rushed around her, blocking out everything
but the feel of rhythmic thudding of hooves on earth,

and the rolling motion beneath her. She began to nod off, but she could not sleep if she was to catch the war party. They would be riding all night, and over the next day or two they would stop only briefly for a little sleep and to rest the horses.

Without halting, she reached into the forward saddlebag for a length of thick leather cordage. She looped it around her waist and lashed both ends to the saddle, just as mothers did to keep children from falling when the village traveled during the night.

Suddenly her face slammed against something solid, and brightness slashed her eyes. She could not find her bearings. Her face bounced against the thing again, and again. It was moving . . . Bull's leg. She was hanging half off her horse. Her hand scrabbled for his mane but felt only stubble. Finally she found the pommel, pulled herself up, and halted.

The sun was high and melting white. She squinted into it and looked about her. She was on a plain surrounded by small mountains, and beyond them stood more mountains, and far beyond them, big, jagged mountains. It looked much like her own valley, and like Where-the-rivers-come-together. But there was no river.

She listened for the rushing sound of water, but heard only the wind's voice. Her eyes found no distant string of trees such as lined rivers in many places.

They must have turned away from the river, for surely they had not crossed it. But in what direction, and how far? The sun was centered in the sky; had Bull been walking the whole time? Probably he had stopped to rest and graze, perhaps for most of the morning. From the look of him, though, he might have plodded ahead without stopping. His breathing was labored.

It was impossible to judge how far they had traveled, or in what direction, or whether they had traveled in circles. Indeed, the river might lie just the other side of this valley.

"I have a plan, Bull," she said, and slid from his back.

She walked him across the valley to the edge of the mountains, and searched the gullies for water. A bright green patch of grass caught her eye and led her to a small marshy area and the trickle of a spring that fed it. She let Bull drink while she uncinched the saddle and packs and checked his back for hot spots.

"I will picket you here," she told him, pounding the stake in the ground. "You can eat while I climb up and look about."

A hard wind was driving over the mountaintop and she had to hold her hair back with both hands to see. In every direction, she looked upon unfamiliar mountains and valleys. Toward where the sun rises, she made out two threads that could have been creeks, and just beyond, a wide river. No river lay in the other direction.

Could Bull have crossed the river? It was raging with spring thaw, but perhaps beyond the forks there was a place where it spread itself wide and thin across a plain, where it would be easy to cross. If Bull had wandered across the river while she slept, they would be on the other side of it now. Then it could be the one she saw.

The girl cursed herself for falling asleep.

Born-great's ghost must be laughing now. She snatched up a rock and hurled it as hard as she could. The rock bounced crazily down the mountainside and ricocheted into the expanse surrounding her.

6

SHE DID NOT KNOW WHETHER SHE WAS DOING the right thing, but now that her belly was full with dried meat she felt emboldened to forge onward.

Even if she could find her way back to the village, what was there for her? Nothing, if she returned with nothing to show.

She mounted Bull and looked about her grimly.

There was still a slight chance she could pick up the war party's trail. No matter what river she had seen, she must ride toward it, for certainly Bull had not crossed the mighty Elk, beyond which the Headcutters lived.

She rode to a pass through the mountains into the next valley and wound her way through a series of little valleys before breaking into the valley of the river. She could now see it was a vast, rolling plain speckled with sagebrush, much like the village's summer camp, flanked far in the distance by mountains. Sage and rabbit brush tingled in her nostrils. Snow lay in large patches on the flattened tan grass like spots on a paint horse. The broad hills seemed to beckon her to gallop across them and whirl about with sheer pleasure at their openness.

She kept a tight rein, however. She did not know what enemies she might meet here—Headcutters or Cheyenne or Blackfoot, or even tribes she had never heard of.

She scanned the landscape. A large herd of buffalo was wallowing downriver, and a few pronghorns stood looking at her. She watched for some time, but saw nothing to indicate the presence of other humans, so she rode out to the river.

It was twenty horses wide and running furiously. She looked to the buffalo again. Where there were this many, enemies might well be concealed nearby preparing for the hunt. She did not want to alarm the animals and thus give herself away, so she followed the river in the other direction.

She saw many tracks in the dried mud—muskrat, buffalo, rabbit, mice, deer, coyote, bobcat, an occasional bear—but no sign of horses. She walked Bull along the grassy bank until it was too dark to distinguish prints from shadows. They spent the night in the open, away from the river. She slept hard, but a nightmare jolted her awake before dawn. She sat up, gasping in the dark, trying to calm herself. It was a familiar dream, in which Born-great was hiding behind their father's backrest with a hatchet, waiting for her to fall asleep. After this dream, she never went back to sleep.

As soon as there was light enough to see by, she started on her way again.

Three more days dragged on. The country was changing now. For long stretches, hills pressed close to the river. Twice she spotted horse tracks, but they were too old to have been made by the war party. Toward evening of the third day, she came to a place where the river forked.

She rubbed her neck, stiff from peering so long at the ground. Ahead, the main river branched off toward the sunrise and was lost in woods and cliffs. She strained her eyes in the gathering dusk. This way would probably be impassable.

She did not think any Headcutters lived this far toward the land of forever summer. With every step she might be riding farther from the trail she sought.

She searched the ground halfheartedly a while longer, until a track stopped her abruptly. She slid to the ground and crouched to examine it more closely. Several indistinct tracks led to this one at the water's edge, printed clearly in wet sand. A large bear had stepped here, recently. The angle of the toes and the long distance between the toes and the claw tips told her it was a grizzly. She pressed both hands into the deep print. A large grizzly.

Fearful of stumbling upon the creature in the dark, she decided to make camp immediately. She snatched Bull's bridle and led him quietly up a long, grassy slope.

When she was satisfied they had left the bear behind, she unloaded Bull in a stand of slender aspen near a stream. A tender spot had developed on his back from the saddle. She packed it with mud and picketed him close by to graze.

The girl was hungry for fresh meat, but only a fool would hunt in strange country after dark with a grizzly roaming about. She sat with her back against a sapling, chewing on dried meat from her pack, feeling tired and sore and discouraged.

The air was crisp. Behind the hills, the horizon glowed turquoise, climbing to green-blue, and overhead, the dark blue just before black. But the colors and the comfort they brought her were soon swallowed in blackness. Through the tiny, fluttering aspen leaves she counted many stars, and felt very lost.

She could not keep on like this. Who knew how long this river was; it might go on for days, or it might fork off again and again until it disappeared in a trickle. She would not find the war party.

Born-great's ghost must be feeling smug.

What was she going to do? She had food left for two, perhaps three, days. Then she could survive for as long as she was able to find game. But still she would be lost. Lost and alone.

"Bull, have I made a mistake?" she asked quietly. "Grasshopper is sorry for calling me an orphan—he stood up and told the entire village that I am a better warrior than Laughing Crow. Would it truly be so terrible living in his family?"

Bull went on grazing.

"Then I would have a mother." Grasshopper's mother was a fat woman who worried a great deal about him.

She thought of her own mother, whom she had never known, but secretly liked to imagine. In her mind her mother was a strong, quiet woman with fine skin and doe eyes, who tied her sleek hair with blue beads, and wore a white antelope-skin dress, and sang the girl to sleep.

A sudden grief for her father washed over her. She pressed it back.

What would she *do* if she lived in Broken Branch's lodge? Just be a girl? She would not even be good at that; girls dug roots and cooked and sewed beadwork and did many other things of which she knew little.

Also, girls courted, and married.

Grasshopper's brother Lies-down-in-water came into her mind. He was good-looking in a quiet way, and surprisingly big when he was near her. She always felt embarrassed around him, although he never spoke unkindly to her. He never spoke to her at all.

"Just being a girl is nothing," she said scornfully. "I could never live like that."

She scooped a handful of water from the nearby rivulet and drank, but not much, for the water was lukewarm and tasted stale. In the morning she would find better water. She would bathe, too. Then she would think of a plan to make a name for herself. She fell asleep trying to imagine her victorious return, but somehow it did not fill the empty place in her.

The birds woke her just as the sky was growing light. Impatiently, Bull snorted to be cut loose.

Very high clouds scudded across the sky, but near the ground the air was almost still. Carrying the saddle and baggage herself, and alert for any sign of humans or grizzlies, she led Bull down to the river. He walked in and drank while she splashed the cold water over his back and wiped off the mud she had smeared on the tender spot.

"I will ride bareback today, and let you heal," she said. He scrambled out of the river and shook himself.

"You look like the horse of an orphan, Bull," she said ruefully, slipping out of her moccasins. He did look wretched, with his raggedly shorn mane and tail and his winter coat shedding in mangy patches. But where the long, dull hair had fallen away, he glowed gold, and his black legs shone like obsidian.

She stripped off her clothing and stepped into the river. The cold took her breath away. She scrubbed herself and dunked her head, and as she lifted a hand to peel her matted hair out of her face she had a strange sensation: her hand felt hot.

She reached out and felt around in the water. In one place the water was hot.

Trailing her hand in the flow of hot water, she waded upstream in search of the source. Against the current it was difficult to keep her footing on the slippery rocks. Just around a slight bend, a steaming-hot creek poured into the river. She yelped and scrambled out of its path.

She climbed out of the river and stood on the stony bank, shivering and dripping, staring in disbelief.

"This must be the Land of Boiling Waters, Bull," she said, and ran to gather her clothes.

7

HEEDLESS OF LAST NIGHT'S GRIZZLY TRACKS AND
the possibility of enemies lurking among the trees and
cliffs, she urged Bull up a steep slope alongside the hot
creek. His saddle bounced awkwardly from the saddlebag strap and to stay on she kept a strong grip on his
bridle. They plunged over the crest of the hill through
scrub juniper, scattering a band of elk.

Two hundred paces ahead loomed a huge, frozen waterfall, solid white and motionlessly gushing over count-
less lumps of stone. But the air was nowhere near cold
enough to freeze a waterfall. And, strangely, smoke or
steam drifted from its crown.

As they approached the base of the strange falls she
saw that water was flowing in sheets over it, and the
thing was not only white, but dripping with yellow,
cream, and dark orange streaks. Water dribbled from yellow icicles into encrusted pools that overflowed into

more and more pools, finally draining into creeks below.

She walked Bull close to a steep face streaming with water. She leaned out and touched it. The water was burning hot; behind it the frozen waterfall seemed made of stone.

She swung far to the side, where the stone became a hill of earth, and Bull clambered up.

On top the hill was the same oozing white. It breathed out foul-smelling steam. She tried to stay upwind of the steam while she explored the hilltop. Was this the place of which Chews-the-bear had told his stories? If it was the Land of Boiling Waters, then she knew where she was. The big river she had been following before must be the Elk. From the Elk, she knew how to get home.

But was this the place? She knew that there should be pools of boiling water and bubbling mud in the area. Trees and mountains around her concealed whatever lay ahead.

One other thing she knew about the Land of Boiling Waters was that somewhere in it stood the black cliff. The thought quickened her senses, and for the first time, she wondered . . . The black rock drew her so strongly it was almost as if it were a part of her that she had been separated from all her life. As if it had been meant for her, not her brother. Could it be?

Perhaps she had been meant to come here. If she had caught the war party, they probably would have allowed her only to fetch water and carry moccasins, not to fight. Perhaps she had been meant to lose her way, to come to the Land of Boiling Waters and find the obsidian cliff. It must be her fate to do something alone, something that would prove she was no lowly orphan, but a great warrior . . . perhaps even the Great One.

"Yes," she told Bull with new hope. "We will search for the cliff."

She headed Bull around the flank of the mountain from which the stone waterfall grew. They walked among huge gray hulks of rock that stood like ghostly sentries on the mountainside, and headed up the bed of a rocky stream that had cut a narrow pass between the mountain and its brother.

Emerging on the other side, she felt as if she had walked into a strange land. An immense green flat sprawled out before her, almost too bright to look at in the sunlight. A single large stand of lodgepole pine stood in the distance. Far away, mountains rose abruptly from the valley floor.

The sun felt warm here and the air was still across the wide flat. Antelope skittered away before them through thousands of little white and blue flowers, and blankets of yellow. White birds of a kind she had never seen before soared overhead, squeaking mournfully.

Along the banks of a small lake she found plentiful mule deer, elk, and moose sign. In the distance, brown spots moved over the meadow.

"Buffalo," she said, yanking Bull's head up from the tender grass. "Surely neither of us will go hungry."

Though the buffalo were far away, she thought nothing of their galloping off as she rode toward them, until she heard a roar and noticed the bears. There were three: a large dark one, a smaller blond, and a smaller brown. A mother with cubs?

She was downwind and the bears had not noticed her. She drew closer. From a stand of firs near the edge of the valley she saw from the dished-out faces and massive humps of muscle at their shoulders that they were grizzlies. The small bears were actually quite large, and the large one was too big to be female. She wondered if he had left the big print by the river. He was dark brown, close to the color of Chews-the-bear's grizzly pelt.

Her eyes narrowed as she thought of returning home with the big bear's pelt on her back. But even she was not desperate enough to attack a grizzly. She watched the smaller bear, a cautious, reddish-blond creature, pad toward the small brown bear. The big brown laid its ears back and growled through bared teeth. The golden bear stopped, then tried again. She decided that they were two males fighting over a female. The golden bear must be a young male with no territory of his own.

The big bear let out a roar, sending the golden bear bolting away a few paces. The big bear charged into him, slamming him off his feet, and gave one heavy swipe at his face before the golden bear galloped away. The big male chased him to the edge of the meadow, then loped back to the small brown bear, licking her muzzle.

Reluctantly, the girl turned away from the grizzlies. Now that the young one had been banished, she might be noticed. She guided Bull into the trees.

She had ridden a long time, out of the main valley, and was exploring along a winding creek when she began to feel drops on her face. Charcoal-gray clouds were seething along one edge of the sky. Suddenly the clouds split with lightning. At the thundercrack, Bull stamped and snorted.

"Easy, Bull," she soothed, looking for shelter. To their left a cliff molded of granite columns rose out of the grassy floor. She dismounted and led Bull through trees and undergrowth in search of a cave or sheltered wall.

With surprising swiftness the dark clouds moved over the valley, and with them came the wind, as strong and sudden as a splash in the face. She found an overhang in the rock, and maneuvered Bull into the space underneath just as rain began to pour from the sky.

The wind whipped the rain into crazy dances, soaking her moccasins and leggings up to the knees in spite of the overhang.

After a moment, hail began clattering against the cliffside like a barrage of rocks, battering their legs. Bull lurched about anxiously and it took all her strength to hold his head.

Then, as suddenly as it had begun, the storm passed over them. The grumble of thunder was audible in the distance, but here the sun already peered down on the glistening grass as she led Bull out. Hailstones the size of acorns lay like sparkling gifts on the meadow.

She reached down to pluck one from the bank of the creek. As her fingers closed around the ice, something else caught her eye. In the sunlight the coarse, wet sand sparkled like shards of obsidian. Black obsidian.

She dropped the hailstone and raked her fingers through the gravel. She looked closely at the black glitter on her fingertips, then the ground around her. There were some rocks of the stuff—and a boulder.

Scrambling over fallen rock, she reached the cliff, and pressed her hands against the rough pillars. They were scaly with gray and bright green lichen, and high overhead the rock was honeycombed and swirled with red, like the marrow of a bone. But if one looked closely, patches of wet black gleamed through. This cliff was not formed of granite at all, but of obsidian.

Now that she knew for certain where she was and how to find her village, she had no intention of going there. She made camp immediately. There was plenty of game here in the Land of Boiling Waters, more than enough to sustain her while she prepared to meet her destiny. For the spirits, she suspected, had led her here, and revealed the cliff to her. What else could explain the sudden rain? Had she not seen that sand while it was wet, she would have walked past it. And if the spirits had led her to the cliff, was it not possible that she *was* the Great One? She barely dared think such things, but something important awaited her here, she was certain.

Whatever it was, she would be ready. She held up the arrowhead she was working on. It gleamed black in the soft evening light with secret power.

"What do you think, Bull?" she called. "These arrowheads have medicine; they will strike anything I aim at."

Bull, grazing across the creek on the other side of the meadow, ignored her. Satisfied with her edges, she laid the arrowhead proudly on a rock next to the others, above her new knife blade. They were jagged and uneven, for she was no arrow craftsman, but they were beautiful nonetheless, like tongues of black fire.

"Tomorrow I will replace my old heads with these, and we will have fresh meat," she announced. Bull snorted. "I know, you don't think much of that, since you won't eat any and yet must carry it."

The next morning, as soon as she had finished her arrows, she went out in search of game. Almost immediately she spotted a band of elk moving like ghosts among the pines. Just as she had boasted, her first arrow found its mark, a young buck, and with a second arrow, she brought it down. More than ever, she saw no reason to thank the animal.

Her new knife blade glided through the buck's hide as though it were mud. She began to hum, then sing about her adventure. She wished she had a good name to sing also, something fearsome. She could not sing of being Weak-one-who-does-not-last.

She unwrapped her fire drill and tinder and soon kindled a clean little flame. While the meat sizzled, she fitted her new blade into one of the buck's short antlers.

The fresh-roasted elk tasted so good she ate too much and made herself sick. She lay in the grass until the worst of the feeling had passed. In the buck's hide she wrapped as much meat as she could fit in Bull's saddlebags. Much of the meat would have to be left behind, but she did not worry; game was plentiful in this country. Bull still flinched when she touched his sore, so she smeared elk grease on it and rode bareback once more. With a kick and a lusty cry she set out to meet whatever enemy the spirits set before her.

The afternoon was cool and gray. They passed through a pine forest and near some strangely steaming, stinking holes in the ground. She stopped to admire a vibrant green-yellow lake, wondering what such water tasted like.

As they approached a bare white patch on a small mountain, steam roared from several holes in its side.

She stood and watched in amazement, but pulled back as she realized the steam was coating her in a smelly film. She rinsed herself in one of the ponds across from the roaring mountain. Not long after, she came upon a spring that sizzled like bear grease on a cooking rock. Bull clomped through a narrow river that rose to his thighs, and they followed its twists awhile.

Then, above the treetops on the ridge ahead, she saw smoke rising. Could this be the enemy she was to brave?

Cautiously she weaved Bull between the pines up the side of the ridge. From the top she could see several columns of smoke. It must be a large party, perhaps a small village, she could not guess of what nation. She tied Bull to a broken tree and crept up on foot. Her heart began to trip over itself as she made her way through the trees over ground turned white and barren.

A sound like a waterfall floated to her. She crawled

over the crest and beheld the source of the sound, and of the smoke.

Before her spread a wet, whitish valley burbling with columns not of smoke but of steam. A small hillside spewed steaming water into the air, as if spitting out mouthfuls of broth too hot to swallow. The place was alive with gurgling and hissing sounds, but empty of life.

She trotted back down to fetch Bull. She was able to mount him easily from the broken tree, and soon they were crossing the barren valley.

Sickly-sweet steam rose in tufts from the pale gray earth, as if fire had just swept the valley, leaving nothing but smoldering ashes. In places the ash-colored earth melted into pale red or darker gray. Rivulets and sheets of water flowed soundlessly from deep, burbling pools.

Some of the pools glowed milky turquoise or bright blue. She urged Bull over to them, but after a few steps across the flat, his forelegs crashed through earth into hot water. With a scream, he reared and shied back. The girl clutched his bridle, managing to stay on his back, but she could not control him. He plunged about in a panic, punching through the crust several more times before he veered onto solid ground.

"Easy, easy," she murmured in his ear, patting his neck. She slipped to the ground and crouched to examine his legs. Fortunately the water had been shallow, no deeper than his fetlocks. Bull stood quietly, showing no signs of pain, while she felt his legs up and down.

"I am sorry," she said, stroking his black face. "This is

a strange kind of land. I must be more careful." She remounted from a fallen rock and gave the center of the valley a wide berth.

Along the edge, though still ashen, the earth seemed solid. Bull walked through a golden river half as deep as his hooves. Ahead they met one of the turquoise pools, glowing like a moon. She wanted to gather all the colors like flowers and hold them against her skin.

She started Bull up the side of the hill. Along their path a small, deep pool of steaming water suddenly belched, as though she had dropped a big stone into it. She squinted at the pool. No stones were being dropped into it, yet it continued to splash. Then, abruptly, it stopped and lay still.

"This valley is a camp of the Great Mystery," she whispered to herself, beginning to feel frightened. "Or of Death. It is not for humans." She urged Bull out of the valley.

From the hilltop she turned and took a long look to burn this place into her eyes. Near the middle of the flat a few dead trees stood like ancient gray skeletons in the white landscape.

She turned and started down a long slope. It was bordered by pine forest but the slope itself was barren except for a few brave clumps of lodgepoles. Sputtering, steaming holes dotted the hill.

On her left spouted a powerful spring, spilling into multicolored gullies down the hillside. Some of the deeper gullies were dry; the spring must once have run quite heavily. Now it was spurting straight into the air, almost even with Bull's knees. She was turning Bull away when she felt a trembling in his body.

Before she could think, a column of water exploded from the earth next to them, bursting high into the sky, raining boiling water on them and blasting them with nauseating steam. Bull shrieked and reared so sharply it seemed he would crash down on her. Falling, the wet reins sliding out of her hands, she grasped at something hard that broke off in her fist, and she landed on her shoulder, crashing through the crust into burning water. She scrambled on all fours through blinding, reeking, hot spray, suffocating in the steam.

Finally she broke through to fresh air. She kept stumbling forward, not stopping until she collapsed on brown earth on the hilltop. Pain seared her skin as she lay gulping air. Water thundered into the sky, towering above the pines. A shift in the wind gusted more boiling rain on top of her, and in terror she scrambled into the trees. The edge of the thicket was all she could manage. She slumped dizzily against a tree trunk.

"Bull! Bull!" she croaked, looking frantically about for him, but he was nowhere to be seen, and her cry was like a drop in a thunderstorm.

9

SHE HAD SEEN PEOPLE DIE, AND SHE KNEW IT WAS happening to her. She felt weak and chilled, her heart beat in trembles, she could not catch her breath. She needed warmth, but her buffalo robe was strapped across Bull's back, and Bull was gone. Gone with her robe, her food, her bow—everything.

She huddled against the tree trunk, struggling not to panic. She needed some kind of covering, quickly.

She tried to focus her thoughts and blot the pain from her scalded arm and shoulder. Her eyes searched the thicket and the hilltop for anything of use.

Water was still blasting from the spring, but only as high as her head. There was a rumbling underground.

An idea came to her. She struggled to her feet and slowly walked across the hilltop. The feathered ends of her arrows, which had broken off in her hand as she fell from the horse, lay scattered across her path. With every step her buckskin shirt, heavy with water, chafed her burns. Holding her upper body as rigid as she could, she staggered to a hot spring. She crouched down and dipped her uninjured hand into the water washing over the rim. Too hot.

But one of these pools might be cool enough to warm herself in. She stumbled down the hill through the pines. She tested pools quickly as she went. All were far too hot.

Though her burns seared her, the rest of her skin was cold and clammy and she had to pause every few steps.

The streamlets running down the sides of the hill were just warm, but they were tiny and shallow. She remembered the deeper gullies she had seen branching out from the angry spring. Water from the spring must be running in them now, and they would be deep enough for her to lie in.

She hurried to the other side of the hill and began climbing up. One of the gullies cut a path through the trees and branched into smaller, steaming streams on the open hillside.

Where the gully forked into streams she squatted and touched the rushing water. Hot, but not burning. She eased her body into the gully, wincing. After a moment the heat became tolerable. She leaned back and let the hot water run over her.

At first, she did not remember where she was or what had happened, but as soon as she tried to sit up, the pain in her arm and shoulder reminded her.

She did not know how long she had been lying in the

ditch. It was dry. Her skin, her hair, her clothes were coated with white scum. The sky was pale pink, but from sunset or sunrise, and on what day, she did not know. Her throat ached with thirst. Water gurgled in pools and rivulets all over the hillside, but she did not trust that it was good to drink.

Her head felt as light as breath when she stood up. She crouched down for a moment to let the dizziness fade.

There had been a river, she remembered. With effort she walked up the hill and down its other side through the pines, trying to retrace her steps. It would have been easier to skirt around the hill, but she thought the trees knew best where it was safe to stand, so she stayed in the thickets.

She called to Bull as she went, hoping he might have circled back, but he did not appear.

Her shirt was dry and had plastered itself to her burned back, shoulder, and arm. She moved carefully to keep it from tearing at her wounds. The sky grew rosy and then blue as she made her way down the white hill, around the edge of the ashen flat, and over the rise to the river. So, it was morning.

Like an old woman with pain in her bones, she knelt stiffly on the lip of the riverbank and scooped water into her mouth, again and again. The water was fresh and cold. She stepped into the river and sucked in her breath as she let herself sink up to her chin, in the hope that wetting her shirt would loosen it from her skin.

The icy water felt good washing over her scalded skin and her bruised shoulder. As the cold numbed the pain, she began to notice the ache in her stomach.

Again it came to her that Bull had taken everything with him. She thought of the broken arrow ends strewn across the white hill. She could use the feathers from these for new arrows. There seemed to be no stone nearby for the heads, but perhaps sharpening the wooden shafts would be enough. What of a bow? She had no sinew, but she could make a fiber cord, and a green branch or a shoot would hold its spring for a day or two—then she could cut another.

If she had her knife. She fumbled underwater and felt the antler handle jutting from her belt.

But there was the problem of her shoulder. Even when it was healthy she needed all her strength to draw a bowstring. Now she had no strength. She thought of Grasshopper and his small, bent arm, and for the first time knew what it was like for him. Were he ever left alone, he would starve to death.

She must find shelter and food. She could make a shelter from pine boughs, if only leaned one against another. But what would she eat? Perhaps she could catch small game. She had always scoffed at the village boys, setting snares for rabbits while she stalked deer and buffalo and bighorn sheep, but even a stringy hare would taste good now.

No berries or seeds or nuts were yet ripe, but there

were always roots. She wished she knew more about what roots to dig and where they like to grow. But that was women's work, much beneath a great warrior like herself, she thought ruefully.

Even an abundance of small game and roots would not keep her alive for long, however. They did not contain enough fat.

The river was growing too cold. It had unpasted her shirt from her skin, and she drew her knife to cut away the leather. The tip of the blade had broken off. Nevertheless, she could cut with it. She was not clever with her left hand, but she managed to slice off the right sleeve and free her shoulder blade.

Her flesh stung when the air touched it. Most of her right hand and arm was red and raw. This must be how her shoulder and right side of her back looked as well, because the air also burned her there. With one hand, she wrung out the sleeve remnant and took it with her out of the water. She dared not throw anything away.

There were tracks by the river telling of buffalo, elk, and other animals that had passed this way. The Land of Boiling Waters was a land of plentiful game, but there would be none for her now. She tried to forget the tracks as she searched along the riverbank for plants to eat. The plants were young, making it difficult to tell one type from another, and it seemed that most of the food plants she knew from her valley did not grow in this strange country.

She was beginning to despair when she discovered some stalks that looked like a plant she knew. But they also looked like another, poisonous plant. She dug out one of the clustered roots and rinsed it in the river, but still she was not sure.

She had little choice. She tore off part of the root and chewed it a long time before she could swallow. It was tough and woody, but the flavor was not unpleasant. Her stomach began to snarl for more, but she must eat only a little at first, in case the plant was poisonous. She dug up all the plants in her path that she recognized as edible, and a few she was uncertain of. She left them in a heap on the riverbank while she wandered off in search of other food.

In the pines along patches of snow she came upon a kind of mushroom she knew. She recognized them easily because they often followed snowbanks and had oddly wrinkled bodies. She popped one into her mouth, but as she bit down she thought again, and spat it out. They must be cooked, she seemed to remember. She made a pouch of her severed sleeve by knotting the bottom, and stuffed it with mushrooms.

She dropped her roots into the sleeve as well and drank again from the river. Drink as much water as you can, the wise ones often said; it keeps your blood thin. She drank some more, thinking that in her situation she should be especially careful to keep her blood thin.

The sun was slanting across the sky, and she had never

felt so tired. She must prepare a fire and cook her food. She must also find shelter before the sun dipped behind the mountains and left the valley dark.

For her fire she cut a willow shoot that she hoped was dry enough for a spindle, and found a fragment of aspen to use as a hearth board. She knelt down, setting aside some dry grasses and bark for tinder, and a few buffalo chips she had gathered.

But even as she placed her hands on the drill she knew she would not have fire tonight, or any night soon. With her wounded arm and shoulder she could not drill with enough power to kindle a fire.

She lowered the sleeveful of roots and mushrooms into one of the boiling pools, hoping this would do. She left them weighted to the edge with a rock while she searched for a place to build her shelter.

She chose a site close by, in a small opening in the woods halfway up a hill near the river. It was difficult to find pine branches, for most were up high on the trunks, where she could not hope to reach with only one good arm. She turned to cutting up the tiny new pines that grew on the fringes of the forest. With her injuries, it was slow, hard work. She dragged the little trees with pitch-sticky hands up to the site of her new camp and tossed them in a stack. The sun set and the valley darkened. She worked as quickly as she could to strip some of the trees and build a crude frame of them. While she struggled to lash the pieces together with baby branches, she thought again of Grasshopper. It was amazing that he managed so well with only one arm.

The dead, steaming flat glowed in the moonlight, and the veins of water running across it shined and murmured all around as she picked her way toward the sleeve of roots and mushrooms.

She was trying to guess how long it had been since her last meal when, looking up from the ground, she saw a bear dipping a paw into the pool. It was the reddish-gold grizzly she had seen driven out of the meadow that first morning. She was close enough to see the muscles in his shoulders rippling as he dragged the sleeve from the water. Suddenly he reared up on his hind legs and circled with his muzzle, seemingly confused by her scent.

She dared not move. No one could outrun a grizzly, and the only trees in the valley were skeletons, dead and nearly limbless. She could not climb them, and there was nowhere to hide.

With a grunt the bear dropped to all fours and, ripping the leather open with a nibble, began to chomp uncertainly at the contents.

"That's mine! Get away from there!" she shouted desperately.

The bear stopped, startled.

The girl was startled, too. Tentatively, she raised her good arm and tried to look menacing. The grizzly weaved uncertainly but did not approach any closer. She roared at him. The bear shook his head like a wet dog, turned, and sauntered away. He splashed through the river and meandered along the other side into the distance.

She stood still until he disappeared over the shoulder of a hill.

There was little left of her meal. The shredded sleeve told of the danger of the bear's teeth. She scraped up the dripping remains.

The scraps of mushroom and roots were soggy and bland, and they bloated her stomach. Exhausted, she crawled under her shelter and, twisting to the left, eased onto her side on the pine-bough bed. The familiar, spicy scent comforted her a little as she lay watching her breath and listening.

The tall, limber pines creaked and groaned with the wind in their crowns. They grunted like bears and bleated like terrified buffalo calves.

She found herself longing to hear the real voice of another living creature. She listened hard for a long time for the howl of a wolf or coyote, but heard nothing.

The spirit who had led her to this place must have been Born-great's ghost. How foolish she had been to hope that any gods would take pity on her. She lay shivering on her side. She had always felt alone in the world, but never so alone as on this night.

10

BACK HOME WITH GRASSHOPPER SHE USED TO play at bringing down birds with rocks, but within a few days her burned skin had turned to rawhide, making it nearly impossible to bend her arm, and, using her other arm, she made wild throws.

Although she spent her days gathering and eating roots and mushrooms and anything else she could find, as one moon melted into the next, her bones rose to the surface and grew heavy. At first she chose her foods carefully. She followed the grizzly's example. When she came across plants from which he had nipped off the tender tips, she tried them. Wherever he had left a few roots behind, she dug them up. She cooked everything she was uncertain of in the hot springs in the hope that this would make it safe to eat. But she did not have the grizzly's acute sense of smell or his powerful shoulders and claws for digging, and as her stomach screamed more sharply to be filled, she no longer concerned herself with boiling, or even sorting poisonous from edible. She ate constantly while she foraged, and her gut was racked with cramps and diarrhea.

Wherever she came upon willows she peeled off the inner bark and ate it. She scraped the pith out of weed stalks, and before long she was eating the leaves and stalks, too. She rolled rocks and logs over in search of ants and grubs. She even welcomed the mosquitoes that attacked her in larger swarms every day, for she slapped at them and ate them, too. She tried to trap squirrels and mice, but she was grateful if she could find their caches of seeds and pine nuts.

For the grizzly often arrived before her. Though she seldom saw him, she often came upon a gaping pit where he had raided some small animal's burrow, or ripped-apart logs emptied of insects, or torn-up earth where great quantities of roots had been devoured.

As if in mockery of her, elk and moose and even deer often passed nearby, and sometimes stopped to graze, grown used to her presence and unafraid. She tried to creep close enough to one of the newborns to attack it with her knife, but each time, the animal seemed to sense her intent and would skip out of reach just before she sprang.

This is what she had come to: a starving wretch un-feared even by infants. She might as well be back at the village fighting the dogs for the camp's leavings. But she would rather starve to death than face the humiliation of going back to her people empty-handed.

One evening she was lying on a slope above the riverbank, unable to force herself to keep foraging, when she heard a great tramping and snapping of branches. With an effort she lifted her head to see the grizzly emerging from the pines a hundred paces down the river.

She was downwind and the bear had not noticed her. She lay still. His reddish-gold coat rippled in the early evening sun as he ambled across the grass and into the river. He slapped at the water for a moment, then dipped his snout in and came up with a flopping brown fish in his jaws. He gobbled it down and splashed about for more.

The girl watched hungrily. Fish! That was the one thing she had not tried. She had never eaten fish, but it took all her strength to keep from plunging into the river after them this instant. She dared not move until the grizzly left.

Although he was not having much success, he was patient. Sometimes he seemed to have trapped a fish under his great paws, and would dunk his head under, but seized only a mouthful of water. His head dipped down again and again and nearly every time came up empty. She saw him catch two more fish, and fought the urge to rush out and rip them away from him.

Finally, as the sun was setting, the bear tired of his efforts and climbed out of the river, shook himself, and lumbered into the brush.

The girl stumbled down the hill and into the icy water. The fish were not easy to see; now and then a gleam caught her eye and she lunged at it. Once, by waiting endlessly with her hands motionless in the water, she touched one, but the slippery creature wriggled out of her grasp.

The sky faded and began to darken, and still she had not caught a single fish. Winded, and shivering with cold, she lay back on the bank to rest, but was so flooded with panic that after only an instant she returned to the hunt with renewed urgency.

She stood peering into the water until the moon rose, and its reflection on the water blotted out the secret world of the fish.

She heaved her body out of the bitter water into the night air. *I am starving to death,* she thought, and was startled to hear her voice. Gasping and shivering, she scrambled on hands and knees over the ground, trying to find something, anything, that had not already been dug out and eaten. She stuffed a fistful of grass into her mouth, but had to spit it out again to breathe. Thoughts, sensations, images spun through her mind: the elk meat she had left behind . . . Bull's snorting . . . Grasshopper's blood-brown moccasins . . . Chews-the-bear's pipe smoke . . . his story of a winter that was so hard the villagers had to eat their dogs, and finally their tepee covers and clothes.

Her clothes—she could eat her clothes! She bit into the remaining sleeve of her buckskin shirt, but could not tear it.

An owl's call interrupted her frenzy.

She crouched as if in fear of an attack. Her eyes darted about the treetops. Born-great's ghost. He was watching her from somewhere high in the pines.

His eerie call floated down to her again.

"Why must you destroy me?" she cried.

The owl said nothing.

"I did not mean to kill you!" she screamed. "I did not know. I was only a child."

She fell to her knees, gulping for breath, clutching her hair. "I was only a child . . . I wanted . . . I wanted it . . ." Her face clenched in a grimace as she let the long-forgotten truth trickle out.

"I wanted that medicine," she moaned. "Not to break it. I only wanted what you had . . .

"It was an accident," she whispered in amazement. "I did not murder you.

"It was an accident," she shouted up at the owl. "You have no right to torture me this way! It's true, I wanted you dead, but I did not mean to do it."

She clawed along the ground until her hand closed around a broken branch. With her uninjured arm she hurled it wildly at the trees. It crashed into some low branches and tumbled back to the ground. But there was a whooshing of great wings above and the owl's moon shadow glided across the ground and up and over her, and disappeared behind.

The wind died, and there was no sound but the muffled rush of the river. Light-headed, she squatted down. Delirious thoughts swirled around her.

A scream jolted her to her senses. There was a crashing, the bellowing of a bear, crunching, and another scream. She strained but heard nothing more. The sounds had come from beyond the little mountain that flanked the other end of her valley.

The grizzly has brought down some game, she thought. Newborn elk, perhaps, or moose? What she would not do for just one mouthful of meat!

She stood up shakily. She *could* have meat. She could take some from the bear. "It is not over yet, Born-great," she whispered, and fighting her light-headedness, she stumbled as quickly as she could along the riverbank toward the mountain.

Although a swollen half-moon lit her way clearly, the sky was growing light by the time she reached the other side of the mountain. The bear had long finished eating, and there was no sound from him. She knew he was resting somewhere near his kill, ready to defend it. In an instant he could be upon her, crushing her neck in his jaws. The risk was dizzying.

But something was forcing her to keep placing one foot ahead of the other. Unsteadily, she walked as silently as she could, searching for tracks, blood, anything that would lead her to the carcass. Over the crest of a ridge, she came upon it: a trail where something had been dragged across the pine needles. Head pounding, she followed the lay of trampled plants to a spot where the grizzly had raked up branches, soil, and leaves to protect his kill. She dropped to the ground, panting. The pile of scraped-up debris lay not twenty paces away. From it jutted the jagged, glistening end of a bloody broken bone.

Water flooded her mouth. She ached to charge the carcass and tear into it with her teeth.

But she did not know where the bear was; she could only pray she was downwind of his bed. Her best chance was to creep up to the kill, quickly cut away as big a hunk of meat as she could, and run.

She slid her knife from its sheath and gathered her courage. Her breath was coming so hard and fast she feared the grizzly would hear it.

She ran to the carcass and clawed away the branches and dirt until she saw hide, and thrust her knife into it.

She froze as if she had plunged the knife into her own body. The hide was buckskin.

For an instant she scraped at the bloody debris, then instead yanked up the jagged bone. It was a completely stripped shin, dangling from the knee by a tendon. Above the knee flapped the remains of a buckskin legging, over a human thigh.

She dashed the bone to the ground in horror, trying to choke back a scream, but it blazed from her throat, and in an instant was drowned in a roar that made urine run down her legs. Thirty paces away reared the grizzly, ears flattened, massive jaws snapping, lips snarling back from dripping teeth. The big beast's eyes froze in a glare as he dropped to all fours and charged.

11

HER LEGS BUCKLED. SHE FELL FACEDOWN INTO the dirt, and tried to curl into herself to protect her guts. Almost before she hit the ground, ivory claws as long as her fingers flashed past her face, and the roar seemed to burst her ears as the bear reached over her body and slammed a paw into her shoulder.

Then there was quiet.

Could it be over so quickly? Her spirit-soul must have slipped away for a time. But she was still in her body, still alive; she smelled the dirt pressed against her face and felt pain in her arm. Was the bear still here? She dared not move, dared not even relax an eyelid to peer through.

Suddenly a low growl vibrated close to her ear. She clutched her breath inside her chest. She could feel her skin prickling and tried to smooth it with her mind. The bear's breath was foul and his saliva dripped onto her neck and ran under her chin. He shoved at her with his muzzle, but, screaming inside, she did not twitch a muscle. The bear jabbed a paw under her hip and rolled her onto her back. *Keep rolling, protect your belly,* she told herself. Everything her father had tried to teach her from the story of his battle with the she-bear rose to the surface of her mind and body. As if from the force of the bear's shove, she rolled back onto her face, coming to rest on the corpse.

She could not hold her breath much longer. Her lungs ached. Still the bear grunted and shuffled around her.

Finally the air burst from her lungs, and instantly she sucked in another gulp and held it, hoping that the heave of her ribs and the tiny rushing sound had escaped the bear's notice.

He let out a bellow and smashed a paw down on her ribs with a crack. Her hands flew to cover the back of her neck just before the bear's jaws closed around it. She screamed as the teeth pierced her hands. She wrenched one free and grasped blindly for her knife.

Seemingly confused by the thing caught in his mouth, the grizzly twisted his jaws and tried to shake her hand from his teeth. With her free hand she found the knife, and fumbled for a grip. She had it. With all her might she drove the blade into the grizzly's throat.

The bear howled with pain. Blindly, she thrust again and again. Blood spurted from the golden fur. She stabbed again and the blade broke off in his neck. The bear shook her hand loose and she jerked it back, scrambling for some other weapon as he bore down.

The girl's hand closed around something—the corpse's

broken shinbone. She wrenched it free of the knee and plunged the jagged end into the bear's gaping mouth, goring the back of his throat. For an instant he stared in surprise and pain, then began choking. He sent up a wailing like all the spirits of the dead, retching and clawing at his face, trying to scrape the bone from his throat.

She tried to scramble toward a nearby pine tree, but the bear lunged after her. In another breath he would crash down on her; she could not possibly escape. Crazily, she tried to burrow into the ground. Her hands struck the corpse and she clutched at it, squirmed under it, dragging it on top of her. The maddened bear screamed and swatted the corpse with such force it knocked her breath out. Snorting and choking, he dragged and batted the body about as if it were a fish, then crushed it in his jaws.

He retched again, spraying blood, and staggered backward.

He had put some distance between them. She leaped for the lowest branch of the pine and clawed her way up. The grizzly bounded to the tree, but she had climbed beyond his grasp. She kept climbing, higher, higher, before she dared stop and cling to the slender trunk, gasping in relief.

The bear's roar seemed to shake the tree. To her horror she realized the tree *was* shaking. The beast was shoving it with his great paws. She clutched the trunk as he rammed it with his bulk. The tree lurched, ripped up at the roots. She screamed as it began to fall. It crashed against some other pines, and she grabbed at one of them and grasped it to her breast, wrapping her arms and legs around the trunk.

Her eyes clenched shut. Above her terrified whimpering she heard noises that sounded like the bear digging. She heard the scrape of his claws, a sputtering in his throat. She heard the thud of his massive body when his legs collapsed under him, and the long rasp that was his last breath.

She did not open her eyes. For a long while she did not move, only clung to the tree like a frightened child to its mother.

Finally, slowly, she let herself down the pine trunk, a little drop at a time. When her feet touched the ground her legs were trembling so violently she crumpled to the dirt.

The bear lay in a heap nearby, motionless and massive as a mountain. A slight breeze ruffled the long grizzled gold hairs on his back. Above the blood-matted fur of his chest his frothy mouth hung slightly open. His eyes stared dully.

She knew the human corpse also lay nearby, but she refused to look where she might see it.

Her burned arm stung where she had cracked the skin bending it. Her side stabbed at her with every breath, and her hands were so bloody she could not see how much was left of either of them.

She crawled to the grizzly and dug her fingers into the bear's blood-soaked throat, searching for the blade of her knife. She could feel a horrible pain in her hands now, but she must have that blade. Gradually she worked it out of the bear's throat.

With the broken blade she sliced off a large piece of her shirtsleeve and wrapped it clumsily over her left hand to staunch the bleeding. The hand must be badly damaged, for she could not feel her fingers.

With her right hand she cut into the bear's side. There was still a thin layer of last fall's fat under his skin, and she scraped some off and shoved the bloody stuff into her mouth. How sweet it tasted. Food! Food! She had all the food now that she could ever eat.

She pressed her hands and face against the bear gratefully. "I am sorry," she gasped into his thick fur. "I am so sorry. Thank you for giving your life to preserve mine."

She gobbled down more of the fat, half choking, trying to swallow too much at once. She could hear herself moaning, and the sound was good, it was precious. It was the sound of still being alive.

12

SQUINTING UNHAPPILY AT THE RAGGED GRAY
blanket draped across a shallow ravine, she wiped the
sweat from her forehead with the back of a bandaged
hand. It was not much of a burial. Underneath the blanket, alongside the remains of the unfortunate man, she
had tucked a package of bear meat and what bits of the
man's camp she had been able to find: a black pot that
smelled of stew, an otter-skin hat, and a pair of hard,
black moccasins.

She could help him no further. She did not have the
strength to bury him properly so that his body would be
protected from scavengers.

But as she frowned at the makeshift grave, an idea
came to her. There was one more thing she could do for
him. With clumsy hands, she wriggled out of her medicine necklace, and laid it across the blanket.

"You are gone, do not turn back," she said. "We wish to

fare well." And she turned to trudge back up the hillside, back to her work.

She no longer needed the necklace. She had more powerful medicine than half a charm. All doubt had fled: Born-great's death had been an accident, and she was the Great One, the one who would number among the greatest Apsaalooka ever to live.

Who could doubt it, after she had killed a grizzly bear! Alone, half-starved, half-crippled, with nothing but a knife she had killed it. No, she was not Weak-one-who-does-not-last. She could do anything now.

Reaching the edge of the ashen, burbling valley, she knelt at the rim of a hot pool, unbound her hands, and eased them into the water. She had lost her little finger and the side of her left hand almost to the wrist, and both hands were purple-blue and riddled with punctures. She leaned into the pool to submerge her burned arm, too. She could still barely believe she had fought with this arm, forgetting the burn, and had not even felt the pain until she had happened to see the deep red splits in the flesh.

It would take time, but it would all heal; she would soak her hands and arm every day, and use them, and before long they would feel almost normal. Her ribs would heal, also. Now that she had food, she would be well again. She was already gaining strength rapidly. Her wounds from this ordeal would fade away.

But her pride would live forever.

It was not the kind of pride she had always expected

to feel. It was not loud and showy, but quiet, infused with regret. The bear was male, not fully grown despite his massiveness. He had been struggling to survive with no territory of his own. It would have been shameful to boast of killing the beast. She understood now how her father had felt about the killing of the she-bear that had attacked him. Before, she had always thought him foolish for his reluctance to tell the story.

"I have earned a new name, have I not, Father?" she asked joyously into the sky. "But what shall it be?" She squatted over the boiling pool, letting her hands dry in the breeze, trying new names aloud to hear if one had the ring of greatness. Grizzly-fears-her . . . Kills-the-bear. Kills-the-bear felt good on her lips, but the name was too much like her father's. She wanted something different from his name, a name all her own.

Skinning and dressing the bear was an enormous task, and she had to do it quickly, before the meat spoiled. She handled the body with unaccustomed reverence. To preserve the hide in one magnificent piece she had to slit it down the belly and legs, then roll the bear back as she split the hide from his flesh. Though she shoved and leaned with all her weight, she could not so much as send a tremor through the carcass. She decided to butcher out as much flesh as she could, then try again. In this way she was able to roll the body slightly, exposing another section of hide, which she sliced away, exposing more meat.

It was a grueling process, and she was forced to rest

often, but she worked as quickly as she could. If she left the carcass for an instant, coyotes and ravens crowded in. She staved them off by piling scraps for them at a distance, and by waving a sharpened pine lance that leaned always within arm's reach, ready to defend against bolder animals. But she feared another bear might smell the carcass and come to claim it from her. Great One or not, she never wanted to battle a grizzly again.

When finally she had removed the heavy skin, she bundled it up, and with great effort prodded it into a tree crotch to be tanned later. She butchered the meat into small sections, and draped the pieces over drying racks she had built of lodgepole saplings.

She turned the strips of meat several times a day, positioning them carefully, for any spot that touched the wood twice might spoil. Each evening she peeled the strips from the racks, wrapped them in her leggings, and trampled on them to squeeze out any remaining blood.

Her days were filled with hard work and pain from her hands and her side, but she relished the pain. It was a constant testimony to her great deed, like a song of glory humming through her day and night.

She ate as much bear meat as she could stomach each day, and with every mouthful she could fairly feel the power of the grizzly seeping into her limbs.

Now that the threat of starvation was gone, her most pressing concern was a good weapon. She climbed back up the bald hill to the place where the water had burst from the earth. She planned to peel the guide feathers off the broken ends of her arrows and use them on a new set of arrows. Though nearby hills and valleys had softened and filled in with greens, this place was still as barren as winter; only lodgepole pines dared approach the summit. She bent down and picked up what remains of her arrows she could find, then stood and peered over the crest at the angry spring, which was spurting mildly. The gray earth was healing where she had crashed through its crust, but her shape was still visible, as were Bull's chaotic hoofprints. What had become of Bull, she was afraid to think. Swallowing hard, she turned away.

With a rock she shattered the bear's pelvis and among the pieces found several shards suitable for arrowheads. These she honed, lashed to willow shoots with moistened bear sinew, and sealed with pine pitch. When the old hawk feathers had been mounted on their new shafts, she had seven arrows.

The bow was not as difficult to make, but it demanded strength. It took her three days to shape and another to dry, and it probably would not shoot with much power. Though day by day the skin of her burned arm grew more pliable, she could not bend it far enough to draw the bow without fear of splitting open the old cracks, so she did not know whether her new arrows would fly true.

Between tasks, as her strength returned, she set about tanning the bear hide. She made a flesher of one of the bear's foreleg bones, grinding notches in one end to form teeth. She stretched the hide across the ground with stakes and scraped her flesher across it until the last bits of fat and meat had been torn away. Each day the hide grew softer as she scraped and kneaded in the bear's liver and brains, and each night she dampened and folded it up to keep it soft.

The days began to grow pleasantly warm, and longer. Now when she soaked her hands and arm at the hot spring, she sometimes withdrew them early, sweating under the combined heat of sun and water. Her wounds were healing, though her left hand was slow to respond to her commands.

She worked with a joy she had never known before; she was working on the thing she had ached for and dreamed of all her life.

Evenings she lay back in exhaustion, planning and dreaming of her triumphant return to her village. She must work hard on her robe and her necklace; she needed a new shirt—there was so much yet to do. And of course a name; she must have a new name. Of all the ideas that came to her, none had yet inspired her. Lying there, she would decide that the right name would suggest itself at the right moment, and eventually she would slide into a pleasantly impatient sleep.

She could not yet use a fire drill, and thus had no fire to roast the meat or to warm her, but she had waited a long time for roasted meat; she could wait a while longer. And although the nights were crisp, they were no longer uncomfortably cold. Fireweed blossoms burned along the forest edges, green berries appeared on brambles, and animals no longer showed themselves during the warm days.

Finally it was time to make the necklace. Her fingers, still stiff from their injuries, stumbled over the grizzly claws, slowly drilling holes with a bone sliver and sand through their knobby ends and again through their middles, so they could be double-strung with sinew. She polished each one against her shirt until it glowed. They were fearsome claws, mostly ivory, with burnt-colored bases almost too dark to catch the light. The front claws stretched as long as her fingers. She laid them out in a half circle as they would appear on the finished necklace, with the largest in the middle. Between each claw she laid a square of the red-gold fur. What a proud necklace it would be!

She was almost ready.

Her hands had healed with mostly small scars, though her left hand missed the little finger almost to the wrist, and had not regained its whole strength. In her side she felt only a thin pain, when she breathed in deeply. Her burnt arm was flexible enough to try her bow, and she was relieved to find the arrows true. The robe and necklace were finished.

Now for a new shirt. She could not return home with a grizzly robe wrapped around the wretched rag she was wearing. She picked up her bow. Also, she must admit, she would not mind tasting something other than bear meat.

Many animals had moved to higher country, following the tender new browse as snow receded up the mountains, and she was out two days before she caught sight of a tiny group of mule deer. She wounded a doe, and spent most of the morning tracking it into a thicket of brambles. She knelt over the weakened creature, which looked up at her with terrified eyes. Self-consciously she said, "Thank you for giving your life to preserve mine."

That night she made fire for the first time since before her fall into the boiling waters nearly two moons ago. She savored the tendril of smoke as she drilled. Gently she scraped the little ember onto her knife blade and slid it into her waiting nest of tinder. Cradling the nest in one hand, she moved her arm in circles from the shoulder until a flicker appeared, like a much-missed friend approaching from a long way off. She laid the nest of fire on a flat stone, rested a few twigs across it, and soon had a comforting yellow flame large enough to cook over.

Her mouth watered at the succulent scent of mule deer flank beginning to roast. She pulled the thick grizzly robe closer about her shoulders as the night air cooled, and fingered the claws that encircled her throat. She could hardly believe these things were real. That she had truly killed a grizzly bear. That soon she would return home the Great One.

I am not no one anymore, she thought, and the idea repeated in her head like a chant: I am someone. I am someone. I am someone.

13

THE GIRL PULLED ON HER NEW DEERSKIN SHIRT
and slipped her bow and shirtsleeve quiver onto her
shoulder. Heaving the bearskin onto her back, and grip-
ping a pouch made of her old shirt and swollen with
dried venison and bear meat, she started walking.

She followed the river, reasoning that she would find
her way back easily.

As long as I do not fall asleep and sleepwalk away from
the river, she thought. She was reminded again of Bull,
and she hoped he had made his way all right and not
fallen prey to some wild beast. He was only a horse, she
tried to tell herself. There were other horses. But these
thoughts only made her heart heavier.

It was a crisp blue day and an easy walk through grassy
flats and pines; even the waterfall she came upon was
easily skirted. But as the sun cast longer and longer shadows, the river began to twist and wind and seemed to be

wearing into a canyon. Both the grizzly robe and her pouch of venison were growing heavier and more unwieldy with each step. She stopped and rolled them into a bundle and lashed it to her back. Standing a little unsteadily under the weight, she surveyed the river ahead, and was beginning to doubt the wisdom of following its meanderings when she saw a thin line of smoke rising above the pines in the direction of the sunrise. Or was it steam? She watched it drift and decided that steam would not hang in the air so long.

Where there was smoke, there might be horses to steal. Her journey would be much easier on horseback, of course, but even more important, stealing a picketed horse from an enemy camp was one of the four steps on the path to becoming a chief. She did not know if she would receive credit without witnesses, but perhaps returning home with a strange horse would be proof enough for the council.

She hurried toward the smoke, abandoning the river for a more direct course. She tramped through the brush, through woods, and over hills, the big bundle shifting awkwardly on her back. Each time the smoke disappeared behind a hummock or bend she ran ahead until it came into view again. It might not last long, and it was her only guide in the search for the person who had made it.

Her thoughts raced as she rushed onward. Only one fire. Just a small party, then, or perhaps even one person.

This would be much easier than stealing horses from a whole village.

She pulled up short at the distant sound of a human voice. She dropped to her hands and knees. Though the sky was still light, the sun was low and it had grown dim inside the forest. Her ears strained for further voices, footfalls, or any living sound. There must be at least one scout lurking among the trees, watching for enemies; she must take care not to stumble upon him. She crept forward.

She could hear several voices now, and ahead she saw a small clearing and movement through the trees. She lay still and watched. In the dusk she made out six different bodies. Suddenly fire appeared and she realized that someone who had been blocking it had stood up. That made seven. Plus any wolves in the woods. What nation were they? She could not see from here. No matter, as long as they had horses.

The horses stood somewhere beyond to her left, where she heard their occasional blowing.

She waited for darkness to settle. The men appeared to be eating, and afterward they talked well into the dark. When some time had passed, a man sitting by the fire spoke to the others and they rose and found their places and lay down for the night. The man by the fire sat up after the others had fallen asleep. She grew stiff and impatient from lying still, willing him to sleep.

Finally he lay down. When she was certain all the breathing she heard followed the deep, slow rhythm of sleep, she eased forward on hands and knees toward the horses. There was no moon, and the darkness at the floor of the forest was nearly complete. She strained to see the outlines of the trees in front of her. Moving slowly, feeling the pine-needled ground ahead to avoid sticks or cones that might give her away, she placed each knee in the handprint before it. She followed the sounds of the horses. After a time, she broke through the pines. Starlight glowed faintly in the clearing, like a mist. A grassy opening ran out one side of the meadow; this would be her escape. She could see the white that dappled some of the horses' coats, and when one tossed its head or gave a shake she could make out the whole animal. They stood in a row, ten or twelve of them, probably tethered together through their bridles.

She would take all of them, she thought excitedly as she stood and walked slowly toward the horses. Not only would stealing all their horses make it more difficult for the men to catch her, but it would make her homecoming even more glorious. She would keep only one and make gifts of the others—then how people would respect her.

She had reached them. She could scarcely believe her luck as they stood quietly while she cut one picket after the other, leaving the long rope between the animals to lead them.

She felt the rope toward its end; she would cut loose the last horse and ride this one in the lead, trailing the others behind her. The animal had no white markings and she could barely see it, like a shadow in the darkness, but its lead was visible, sweeping to the ground like a strand of spiderweb reflecting the starlight. As she bent to cut it, the horse snorted and sank its teeth into her buttock.

Stifling a cry, she snapped upright, bumping her head against the beast's jaw. "Bull?" He snorted again. She felt along the animal's neck to its back. Too high for her to mount without a leg up.

"Hush, Bull, quiet!" she whispered, her joy swallowed in fear.

A foreign voice rang out from the woods, answered by two or three others from different depths, like echoes. The wolves had heard. She slashed through Bull's lead and tried to swing the horses around toward the opening in the trees. She could hear the wolves crashing toward her on all sides and the men in camp awakening as she wedged her body between Bull and the next horse and heaved herself onto the smaller one's back. She vaulted from the small horse to Bull and kicked hard. Bull leaped almost out from under her and struck a gallop toward the opening at the other end of the meadow, while the other horses jerked along behind them.

The men had guessed her route and shouted as they raced to cut her off. Two already stood waiting at the mouth of her escape.

"I am the Great One!" she yelled, and bore straight down on them.

The other horses swung alongside as they charged

through the opening. A hand grasped at her ankle but was ripped away as she galloped past. She knew arrows must be flying around her, but she looked straight ahead.

Behind her the sharp voices trailed away.

But suddenly the grassy channel narrowed into an upward draw, and she realized the horses could not pass through abreast. She urged Bull faster, trying to break ahead and string the animals out one after the other, but Bull was not fast enough. The space was closing. She reached over to cut the line that tied her to the other horses. There was a great whinnying and screeching as the horses tangled and collided around her. Just as her blade touched the rope she was jerked over it. She felt Bull falling away as she was thrown over his head.

Even as the heels of her hands struck the ground and she tumbled headfirst over onto her back, her body knew what to do, and as she rolled over onto her feet she sprang upright, and stumbled into a run. She forgot horses; escape was all now. Her feet were light and she ran like a jackrabbit, swerving around trees she could see only an instant before crashing into them.

Suddenly she realized how she was running so easily: there was no heavy bundle slapping against her back. Her grizzly robe! She staggered to a stop and whirled around, eyes frantically raking the ground, but she could hear human footsteps galloping toward her, and in agony, she turned and sprinted up the draw.

It grew steeper and rockier, until she was no longer

running, but clambering up a rocky slope. Soon she was clawing at sheer cliff. Trapped.

Balancing against the wall, she jerked an arrow from her quiver and in the same motion strung her bow, but as she turned to face the enemy, someone swatted the bow out of her hand and raised a skullcrusher over her head.

Just as it began to descend, she slipped her feet off their precarious footholds and let herself fall down the rocky slide. The crack of the stone skullcrusher against the cliff reverberated like a thunderclap. She tried to keep her feet beneath her, but they caught and pitched her into a roll over the rocks and she did not stop until she slammed sideways into a man's legs. He staggered back, almost falling, then nudged her motionless body with a foot, as if to check whether she was dead.

The grizzly attack flashed through her. If I play dead, will they leave me alone? she wondered. She tried not to move as he rolled her onto her back, but she could not stop gasping for breath. She could hear or feel the footsteps of the other warriors approaching. Excited voices ricocheted off the rock walls so that she could not tell where the speakers were. She opened her eyelids just a slit.

An iron hatchet was slicing toward her head.

Before she could throw herself out of the blade's path, a fist flashed out like a rattlesnake and snapped up the handle, halting the hatchet's plunge in midair. Sharp words were exchanged. Her eyes were wide open now.

Two or three men were peering down at her in the darkness. The man who had stopped the hatchet wrested it away and, speaking angrily, thrust the blade toward her chest. She flinched, sucking in her breath. A third warrior poked his bow under her bear-claw necklace. They seemed to be arguing.

A torch was handed forward and the men hovered over her. They could see her better now, as she could see them. Their faces and shaved heads gleamed in the harsh yellow light. They were Pawnee.

In terror she remembered having heard from some Shoshone traders that the Pawnee cut out the hearts of captive girls.

It's just an old tale, just a tale to frighten children! she told herself frantically, struggling not to lose control. I am the Great One. I fear nothing.

The man with the hatchet seemed to be speaking to her. She did speak a little Pawnee, for there lived in her village two women and a boy who were once Pawnee, and she had learned some of their talk. But she pretended not to understand. Now he was making signs, asking something. She would never convince them that she did not understand sign language, for all Plains people knew it, but she avoided answering until he squatted down and made the signs right in her face: *Question— you female?*

She looked him in the eye and signed, *Yes.*

14

ABRUPTLY THE WARRIORS SEEMED TO BREAK INTO good humor. They talked with hands on one another's shoulders as they walked back toward their camp.

The man who had saved the girl's life grasped her hair, twisted it twice around his wrist, and dragged her to her feet. He placed his hand on her head, lifted his face to the sky, and spoke briefly in measured tones, as if praying. Then he tied her wrists in front of her and led her back to the meadow, where the others had rounded up the horses and were already breaking camp.

They set off in darkness toward the sunrise. One of the Pawnee mounted Bull, and their captive was hoisted atop a roan pony lashed between the horses of two others. Through her fear pounded one thought: she must retrieve the grizzly robe. Anxiously she scanned the starlit ground. One of the warriors riding beside her looked at her as if she were making him nervous. Just then she caught sight of a light, shapeless mass.

"My robe!" she shouted, leaning toward it.

The horses started and the Pawnee spoke angrily. Someone near the front maneuvered his skittering mount to the object, swung down to examine it, and scooped it up. Raising it over his head, he gave a victory trill with his tongue and brought the robe over for his fellows to admire. As she watched desperately, he draped the hide across his horse's withers.

"That's mine," she said.

Someone spoke evenly, and several of the warriors turned to look at her. Though she could not make out their expressions in the dark, a cold feeling crawled into her that she had better keep quiet.

Everyone seemed tired, and soon a silence settled over the party. The tedium of horses plodding in darkness gave her time to think.

They must be taking her to their village. To be killed? Enslaved? Adopted? Married? The possibilities whirled through her mind. One of these awaited her, she was certain.

She had nothing to fear, she reminded herself; she was the Great One. She wondered for a moment whether Born-great was responsible for her capture. But his ghost was gone; she felt it. The owl had flown away that night and she was certain that he would not return. She must concern herself now with living enemies.

She would escape. But she could not go dashing off only to be cut down like a frightened rabbit. She would wait for the right moment, when she could escape with her robe. Until that moment came, she must keep her eyes open and remember the terrain so she could find her way back.

As the sky began to lighten she looked about her. They were traveling along a creek through pine forest, occasionally skirting dense stands of spruce. Discreetly she searched out her robe. It had been tied over a mare's rump, and hung down so that the horse's hocks bumped it as she walked. On the mare sat a different man from the one who had claimed her robe last night—the one who had saved her life.

He was about thirty winters old, and he appeared to be the party's leader. He had a sharp nose and a generally sharp look about him, and was dressed very strangely. A hawk hung from the right shoulder of his shirt, and from his left shoulder bounced what she thought was an ear of corn. She had seen corn once in a Big Belly trader's pack, but that was for eating, not wearing. He wore an otter collar around his neck and a twisted-hair belt. His cheeks were painted with red streaks, and his forehead with a red bird's foot. He carried his pipe in one hand while he rode, instead of putting it away.

The Pawnee numbered eleven. She wondered uneasily from which one she had escaped the skullcrusher. Her eye caught the motion of an iron-bladed hatchet slapping against the flank of the horse tied to her left.

On her right rode an old man with a gray scalp lock

and a thick scar across his throat. He must be a man of importance, for had he been Apsaalooka he would have been considered too old for a raiding party. He seemed to feel her gaze and turned to meet it with kindly, wet eyes. Quickly she looked away.

The forest went on and on, and though the earth swelled into hills, the terrain looked like a hundred other places.

The Pawnee veered away from the creek up a steep hill, and at the crest stopped to gaze out over a towering waterfall plummeting like a cloud out of the sky into a gargantuan yellow canyon. She now knew where they were. The Elk River was well known for its wondrous falls, and for the yellow stone through which it had carved its bed.

They rode down to join the river well upstream of the falls, where it flowed wider and gentler through a broad valley. Occasionally the water drowned a flat into a marsh, where grasses and reeds brushed against the horses' bellies and ducks burst from under them. Although they saw moose, deer, and elk, the Pawnee were not interested in hunting. They hurried ahead, in a manner that worried the girl.

They rode past a group of mudholes and hot springs, forded the river, and continued following it to where it gushed from a lake so large that at times she could not see the other side. Then they wound their way between steep, forested mountains and picked up the trail of another river.

On and on they traveled. She ached from her bruises, and her hands were sore with being tied, but she was comforted by the knowledge that as long as they rode, she would stay alive. The sun arced over them and began its descent. The Pawnee never stopped. If one was hungry he simply leaned over, reached into his saddlebag, pulled out a new moccasin, and ate the food that had been packed inside. The old man offered her pemmican and sandy lumps she did not know were food until he signed that they were made of corn. The lumps were dry and flavorless, but she was hungry.

When they came to a grove of aspen, she made signs to the hatchet owner and the old scar-throated one that she needed to pass water.

The party halted and dismounted. Some spread robes and sat down to eat. Strong hands hoisted her from the roan to her feet. The scar-throated man followed her into the trees and untied her hands.

He said something to her in a startling voice that was really two voices at once, a sort of squeak above a deeper, gritty voice.

She squatted and worked her breechcloth aside.

They did not stop again until long after dark. For sleeping, they tied one of her wrists to the two-voiced man, and the other to the hatchet owner. She was awakened what seemed an instant later to push ahead in the darkness.

On the second night, as they were saddling their horses, the animals began to whimper and tremble. The leader's mare and a paint gelding collapsed to their knees and rolled in agony. The girl saw Bull straining his head back to chew at his saddle, and she walked toward him.

The two-voiced old man followed on her heels and with a hand on her arm pulled her around.

"The saddle is hurting him," she said in Apsaalooka.

The other warriors watched warily. Apparently none of them understood Apsaalooka, but Two-voices was trying.

They are in pain, she signed, nodding her head toward the other horses. The men looked at her and one another. "Take the saddles off," she demanded. "It will not hurt your buttocks to get a little sore."

The sudden pinched expression on Two-voices' face told her he did understand Apsaalooka. She blanched, expecting a blow, but he turned to consult with the sharp man. The leader was obviously displeased, but he shouted something at his men, and to her amazement, the saddles were removed. She wondered if these men somehow understood that she was someone to be respected.

They kept the same grueling pace for days, stopping rarely except for a brief rest at night. Two-voices never left her side. Traveling by day, by night, by night and then again by day, with so little sleep, she lost track of time. One landscape blurred into the next, and she began to pick out one big landmark for every stretch they traveled during light, something that could be seen from a distance—a river, a mountain. She would wait until they had passed it and crane her neck around and look at it until her eyes burned.

The warriors must have guessed what she was doing, but they made no attempt to stop her—perhaps because the notion was so ludicrous that she would escape to see that mountain or river again.

Soon the mountains and trees gave way to long, flat hills, spiked with tough grass, cactus, and sage. They rode for two or three days through this barren land, along a shallow river. Then the scrub turned to long prairie grass, and that evening she spotted a huge rock formation. As they approached, it took the shape of a big bluff, thrusting out of the plains. Beyond it a tall spike of rock jutted into the sky like a giant lodgepole. These cheered her, for they could be seen at least half a day away, and could never be mistaken.

That evening, she realized how important those rocks would be to finding her way home, when they turned away from the river, past the bluff and the giant lodgepole, away from all landmarks.

Dawn revealed only an endless prairie of grass, waving in the wind, rolling as far as the eye could see. All she had to guide her now was the direction of travel: toward the rising sun.

The horses were tired, and the heat and lack of water added to their discomfort. The next night the sharp-faced leader allowed the party to sleep almost until sunrise.

They were riding again by the time the Morning Star began to fade. Although she was exhausted, the warriors' manner snapped her fully awake. Something was about to happen.

Not far into the morning the leader slid off his horse, and lifted the pipe he always carried in his left hand. The other men also dismounted, and two of them kindled a flame and held it to the grass. The fire licked across the prairie for a time before withering out, leaving a swath of charred ground.

The men thrust their hands into the still-smoking grass and smeared charcoal on their faces. Then they sprang onto their horses' backs, and with a great shouting raced off with her on the trail of the fire. This could mean only one thing: the Pawnee village was over the next rise.

15

OUT OF BIG, ROUND LODGES THAT LOOKED LIKE hills the Pawnee people streamed, shouting as they ran. The warriors trotted their horses into the center of the village.

As the crowd closed around her, she half expected to be jerked from her horse and killed, but no one touched her. They stood back slightly and fell silent, as if in fear or awe. All eyes followed her as she passed. Perhaps they were staring at the sight of the grizzly-claw necklace hanging on such a slight girl. She straightened her shoulders, trying not to show fear.

The party advanced through the village and halted before the lodge of a man with a slight leering smile on his lips. They dismounted, and the sharp man draped the grizzly robe across Bull's back and led the horse forward. The leering man looked Bull and the robe over as if he had just bought them. The girl watched helplessly, but sure of at least one small satisfaction as the man bent to tether Bull by his lodge. The man let out a most undignified yelp as Bull's teeth sank into his buttock.

The sharp one and Two-voices escorted her through the tunnel-like entrance into the dark lodge. Bull's new owner followed, carrying the robe, still leering in spite of the bite. When he walked up and stood nearly touching her, she realized that he was not smiling at all. Something was wrong with his face that made his lips curl upward.

He sent away several women and children who were inside. The lodge was strange to her; it was a big dome, like the night sky, much larger than a tepee, large enough for thirty or forty people to live in. Except for a pillar of light in the center pouring through a smoke hole onto a fire pit, the lodge was dark.

She watched her robe as the leering man set it on a bench against the wall. He knelt by the fire pit, scraped away the ashes, and with his breath awakened the coals into flames. He stoked it into a large fire, and the girl now saw that the fire pit was surrounded by a ring of tree trunks reaching to the roof. Many more tree trunks circled around the edge of the lodge, supporting a ceiling of woven saplings and thatched grass.

All were silent. With long fingers the leering man unwrapped a large hide. The sharp man handed him the pipe he had carried. The ear of corn and the hawk were cut off the sharp man's shoulders, the hair rope untied, and all placed reverently on the hide. The leering man tied them into a bundle and placed it on a platform against the wall opposite the entryway. It was a sacred bundle, she realized. The man who always seemed to be smiling must be a priest.

The men seated themselves around the fire, waiting for something.

A boy burst into the lodge. Two-voices gave him a stern look and said something in his odd-sounding way. The priest stood, lit a bowl of buffalo fat and sweet grass, and held his hands over the smoke. He beckoned her with spidery fingers to move forward through the smoke to the sacred bundle. Then he bade the boy walk through the smoke.

Was she to be married to this boy? It seemed the only explanation. But why had all those men journeyed for so many days to capture a bride for this boy? Why didn't he marry one of his own kind?

Perhaps there was something wrong with him. He was about her age and, like her, tall, though not as thin. Like the men, he wore his hair almost completely shaven— nothing was left of it but a stripe sticking straight up in a roach from his forehead to the nape of his neck, where it grew gradually longer and hung like a crest of feathers. His large, long-lashed eyes looked girlish and frightened, she noticed disdainfully. He smiled out of the corner of his mouth at her. She looked away.

The two-voiced old man might have been the boy's father or uncle, for he came and stood next to the boy with a hand on his shoulder and seemed to be reassuring or instructing him. The boy looked up at the old man with pride.

The priest opened the sacred bundle and removed a pot of red powder. He mixed the powder with fat and, using a hide dauber, rubbed this grease-paint on her arms. She struggled angrily, but the sharp man and Two-voices held her firmly. The priest reached out to smear the red over her face and she squirmed, trying to turn her face away, but the sharp one gripped her tight by her hair. As the priest daubed down her nose and around her mouth, she sank her teeth into his hand. The sharp man jerked her head back and hissed something in her ear. She did not understand most of the words, but his meaning was clear. She stood still.

The priest reached into the bundle and pulled out a calfskin dress, the twisted-hair belt, a breathfeather, and a pair of black moccasins. He untied her wrists so she could remove her clothes and pull on the dress from the sacred bundle. Rubbing her sore hand, she did as she was bidden. The hair rope was tied about her waist, the moccasins put on her feet, and the downy feather laid on top of her head.

After retying her wrists, the priest fetched a buffalo robe and held it out to her. She hesitated, pointing at her grizzly robe and then at herself.

The priest's gaze was flinty.

She burned inside, but reached for the buffalo robe.

The priest handed the boy a small bowl and buffalo-horn spoon, and spoke to him as though instructing him. The boy held them out to the girl, but she refused to take them, so he carried them himself. The priest turned away and spoke with the sharp man, as if he considered the others dismissed. The two-voiced man whispered to the boy, and the boy silently took the girl's arm in his hand and led her out of the lodge.

He had a weak grip and his hand was probably sweating so much she would feel it through her sleeve in another moment, she thought. She could easily have broken away and run, but there was nowhere to run to. All around them moved curious people, offering what seemed to be encouragement or congratulations as they passed. Beyond the people and their earthen lodges lay nothing but the river and endless prairie.

The boy took her into another lodge that must have been his own. They were alone. He looked at her uncomfortably. He untied her hands, and asked in sign whether they hurt, but although they did hurt her, she only glared straight ahead.

The boy pointed to a platform against the wall piled with robes, and motioned for her to sit down. She thought he would try to touch her, and wondered what to do if he did. But he did not touch her. He filled her bowl with stew and set it and a piece of red corn bread in front of her, then stood back.

She was hungry, but she did not want to show it. She

kicked the food away, sloshing stew over the boy's moccasins. He pursed his lips, but did nothing. The girl sneered at his weakness. He sat down across from her and nervously smiled his crooked smile. For some reason it enraged her.

Pointing to himself, the boy said something in Pawnee that must have been his name, then signed, *Question— you called?* She ignored him. He slid an arrow from a quiver that hung on the wall behind her, and knelt down and began drawing in the hard dirt floor. He talked freely as he carved out figures.

He is friendly because he does not want trouble with his new wife, she thought. *But trouble is exactly what he will get. When I leave this village I will take his scalp with me.*

A big-boned woman, sturdy and peaceable-looking, appeared in the doorway. She stopped short at the sight of the newcomer, and a shadow crossed her face. The young children who had been swept in with her clung to her legs. She shooed them to the far side of the lodge, where they entertained themselves with husk dolls.

More people followed—three young men and old Two-voices, and children, and several women carrying water in leather bags swinging from saplings across their shoulders.

The same shadow of discomfort darkened the face of everyone who entered, but just as quickly it was gone. The older women fell to preparing the midday meal, while the young women looked after the men and the grandmothers looked after the children. Pleasant chatter hummed through the lodge.

The sturdy woman handed her a disc of fried bread as casually as if they were mother and daughter. She took the steaming bread automatically. The woman gave the boy a disc of bread, too, and he bit into it with a show of pleasure, which made the woman smile. She nudged him in the ribs with her foot before walking away.

The boy said something after her that made everyone in the lodge laugh. He tore off another mouthful and chewed as if he had never tasted anything so delicious, surely for the stranger's benefit. She was disgusted. Still chewing, he motioned to her to put the bread in her mouth.

Instead she dropped her bread on the bed and ignored it. The boy frowned, but picked up his arrow again and began drawing where he had been interrupted, babbling in Pawnee.

She paid no attention. She thought only of escape. After a time, reasoning that she would need energy for the journey ahead, she reached reluctantly for the bread and what was left of the stew. It was a concoction of crunchy corn kernels, sweet, with leathery orange strips of something and dried buffalo stomach lining, and though it tasted strange, it seemed to light a flame under her hunger.

The boy was pleased she had decided to eat, and he fetched her two fresh helpings and a new disc of pan-fried bread. As she slurped up the stew she tore off chunks of red corn bread and fried bread and pretended to eat them, too. But whenever the boy looked down at his pictures she tucked the bits of bread between the robes of the bed.

After she had eaten her fill, the boy took her outside and led her across a hill into a big flat, talking all the while. Eight or ten other boys were playing at throwing dull-headed lances through rolling hoops while they ran alongside. They glanced at her uneasily, but swarmed around the boy and laughed and pressed their lances into his hands. Next to his friends he seemed even taller. He did not want to play the hoop game, but the boys cajoled until he took up a lance.

He threw about fifteen times, never coming near the little hoops the other boys gleefully rolled for him. Finally he launched a shot so wild it sailed into the crowd. Amid howls of laughter a chubby boy staggered forward, holding the knobby end of the spear against his belly, and fell on his back.

She was appalled at such horrendous shooting, but the tall boy showed no embarrassment. He marched over, pushed a foot down on the "dead" boy's chest, and, pulling the lance, made a very stern, proud face. Amid cheers he tugged a beaded armband off the "dead" boy and swaggered away, thrusting his chest and his lower lip out, admiring his booty. The "dead" boy scrambled after him, but he skipped out of reach.

Just as his victim was beginning to grow truly angry,

the tall boy laughingly tossed the armband at him, and they kept walking. She wondered at the tall one's undignified behavior.

A third boy caught up to them, and the tall boy signed to her, *We are going to guard the horses.* They followed a path through the grass and splashed across a shallow part of the river to a plain where the horses were grazing. The boys lay on the riverbank. She stood peering out at the herd to see if Bull had been turned out with them. She felt a tug on her skirt.

The tall boy was pointing down the flat to an isolated gold blur with its legs and head buried in the grass. *He had to be staked away from the other horses,* the boy signed with mischief playing around his mouth. *I hear he bites, like his owner.*

Blood rushed to her face and she quickly sat on the ground, trying to maintain a cold expression.

The boys talked and laughed the rest of the day away. Sometimes she saw them looking at her while they talked in low voices, and she knew they were speaking of her.

She worried as she watched the sun set. What would happen when they lay down that night and her new husband tried to touch her? She imagined untying her buffalo-hair belt, slipping it around his gawky neck, and strangling him. The thought crept to her lips in a smile. The boy mistook her smile as meant for him, and smiled back at her. She punctured him with a scornful glance.

But that evening, after the fire died down and the people in the lodge drifted off to their beds against the walls of the great dome, the boy did not lie down with her. He retied her hands for the night, then went to his own bed along the wall.

Her pride stung. If she was not this boy's bride, what was she? His sister? Remembering the carvings on the floor, she rolled over in bed and peered down at them by the moonlight from the smoke hole. For each new picture the boy had scraped away the previous one to clear the floor. The only remaining drawing was of a wolf and a star, connected by a clean curve. It was well drawn; she could see that the animal was not a coyote or a dog, but a wolf. Wolf star. Perhaps it was the boy's name.

It meant nothing to her. The aroma of fried bread sifted through the robes as her face pressed against them. I could leave now, she thought. No one is watching. Despite her exhaustion, energy swelled in her. She peered around the lodge; no one stirred. The boy's knife hung in its sheath on the wall over his bed, beside the entrance tunnel.

Yes, she could do it now. She would strangle her keeper, take his scalp, and escape. Noiselessly she rose and slid an arrow from the quiver hanging beside her bed. Kneeling, she clenched the shaft between her knees, hooked the thongs that bound her wrists under the arrowhead, and slowly sawed them through. She slid a hand under the bed robes and clawed out every morsel of bread, stuffing it down the front of her dress. No sound or movement came from the others. The corn bread scratched at her belly as she picked her way across the big room, to the boy.

She stood over him. Her fingers trembled as they loosened the knot in the hair rope cinched around her waist, and slowly slipped it off to wrap around his throat. Suddenly an avalanche of corn bread tumbled from her dress onto the boy's chest and face. Foolish dress! She was not used to the things. Amazingly, the boy went on sleeping.

But then her eyes caught a quivering about his eyelids. The left side of his mouth was also trembling.

He was trying not to laugh. The boy was awake; he had been all along. What a fool she had made of herself! She raced back across the big lodge and dove onto her pallet.

The boy did not rise. She burrowed into the covers and struggled to collect her dignity. She had been rash, she told herself, she was not ready to escape yet; she would need more food than one day's bread, and in any case, after the hard journey she must build up her strength. Her injuries were almost healed, but best to wait until she was completely fit. Food and rest were what she needed. Yes, she needed more time. She scraped around the dirt floor and her bed robes for the thong pieces, tied them back together, and then worked at retying her wrists. She lay back, wondering why the boy had feigned sleep, when he might have humiliated or even killed her. Gradually exhaustion swept over her like a blanket laid over a sleeping child.

Next morning not a crumb remained on the floor by

the boy's bed. When the boy untied her hands for the day, he acted as though he did not notice that the thong was now several knotted pieces. At the morning meal he said nothing to her, simply carried on a banter with his family, delighting the grandmothers and the young children with his jokes. She was relieved that none of his jokes seemed to be about her. Not until they were alone, walking out to meet the sunrise, did he speak to her. She could barely make out his hands forming signs in the dimness to explain his Pawnee words.

You are thinking of escape, he signed, still walking. *It would be impossible—unless one of us were to help you.* He stopped and gazed into the brightening horizon, where the Morning Star blazed low in a green sky. He turned to face her. *If you try it, they will hunt you down.*

She flinched. With a smile, the boy began walking again. *You will like it here in our village,* he signed, as the red sun peered over the horizon and shimmered on the river.

16

THAT DAY THE PEOPLE BEGAN PREPARING FOR A buffalo hunt. Men took bundles of dogwood shoots to the arrow makers. Women cut elm and willow saplings at the river for their tents, and began to sew new moccasins.

Pretending not to, the girl watched the bustle. Nearly everyone seemed to be planning to go on the hunt, except the very old and the wives and children of some poor families who had too few horses to take them along. In Two-voices' family only the good-natured woman and the boy Wolfstar did not appear to be packing their things.

This was good. It seemed she had been not married, but adopted into the lodge of Two-voices, and Wolfstar was to be her keeper until she lost the will to run away. Her hands were usually untied during the day, although the boy was careful to tie them as soon as the daylight began to fade, before darkness made escape possible. Always Wolfstar was with her; and everywhere he went she was made to go also. If he was staying home from the hunt, the girl was certain that she was staying, too. That meant that when the hunting expedition left, probably before the next moon, only he and a few women and children would stand between her and freedom. She could wait.

Wolfstar led her about the village, pointing out things and people, talking about them in sign language as fast as his speech. She paid little attention, occupying her thoughts instead with escape and the details of her glorious return to her village. But Wolfstar was always with her, always talking, disrupting her thoughts.

He had been adopted so long ago that he could not remember ever not being Two-voices' son. The good-natured woman was his adoptive mother, Her-corn-says-so.

Wolfstar did not call her Her-corn-says-so, he explained. He called her *atira,* because she was his mother, but others called her whatever kin she was to them. She had a personal name that had a special meaning, something only she knew. The Pawnee kept their personal names to themselves.

Vaguely listening, the girl thought about her own personal name. It still had not presented itself. Perhaps it would spring from something yet to happen, something about Pawnee scalps or horses . . .

Reading her expression, Wolfstar asked her name again. But she did not answer.

Every dusk, Wolfstar bade her collect her wooden bowl and buffalo-horn spoon, and took her to the sharp man's lodge for the evening meal. The sharp man had a striking young wife, and a long name the girl did not understand, but mostly he was referred to simply as Dreamer.

Wolfstar did not eat much, but passed the time watching his hands twist the leather lace of his moccasin. He exchanged few words with Dreamer, and when he did his voice was like the edge of a stone blade. She wondered why Wolfstar disliked Dreamer.

The man praised and fawned over his young wife, Hummingbird-in-her-hair, but he seemed to cherish not so much her as the admiration and envy she could bring to his household.

And certainly she could bring much of those. She had melancholy eyes and the elusive beauty of an antelope— graceful and gentle but untamed. She was not quite plump. Her long black hair fell in a thick braid down her back, fastened with a shiny clip. She weaved among them silent as smoke, refilling bowls, and signing to the newcomer with hands like butterflies. She could not have been older than thirteen or fourteen winters, but her eyes were the eyes of an older woman.

The girl had never cared much for others of her sex, yet she felt a kinship with the Pawnee girl that she could not explain. Hummingbird-in-her-hair was her enemy; and certainly they were as unalike as could be—she herself was rough and rawboned and as tautly strung as a hunting bow—yet somehow, it seemed, they were alike. She found herself looking forward to the evening meal.

Often Wolfstar would go out to tend one of the women's crops, and she accompanied him to the fields, which lay in strips beyond the village, separated by fences of tall flowers with big, round heads and yellow petals like the rays of the sun. She had never seen the Pawnee plants before. In her country they did not exist; here they stood in great crowds. But after the first moment they were nothing to look at. They did not give her the special feeling that colors or mountains or the Land of Boiling Waters gave her. Wolfstar, however, never tired of looking upon them or telling her about the different kinds of food that would grow from them, like a proud father expecting grandchildren. Whenever he rested from working the soil or hauling water from the river, he contemplated these fields as if they were the Great Mystery itself, and when he spoke the names of the plants he seemed almost to sing.

One morning the girl awoke late. She sat up, squinting at the brilliant light pouring down through the smoke hole, and rubbing her eyes with her tied hands. She had slept until the sun was high, and Wolfstar had not awakened her. Her gaze darted around the big lodge for Wolfstar, but he was gone. Her-corn-says-so noticed that she was awake, and ambled to her bed.

As soon as her hands were untied, the girl signed jerkily, *Where is Wolfstar?*

A puzzled frown creased the woman's face; then her eyes lit up. *My son will return soon,* she signed. *Come, bring your bowl.*

The girl sat cross-legged at the edge of the fire ring with her cold soup, ignoring the children cavorting around her, and jabbed her spoon at the layer of fat floating in it. She was irritated with herself for missing Wolfstar.

A shadow fell across her soup and legs, and she looked up in astonishment. Peering into the sunlight, she saw a black figure leaning over the smoke hole, wriggling its arms. Wolfstar's voice called down, but she could not understand. If he was making signs with his words, she could not see them; the sun stung her eyes. Her-corn-says-so signed across the fire pit to her: *He says, guess what he has.*

I don't care, she signed back.

He says it's your bear, and if you don't catch it, it will land in the ashes.

She looked up to see Wolfstar lowering the robe through the smoke hole as if to drop it. She leaped up into the fire pit, knocking soup and bowl across the floor, and throwing her hands out in front of her. The grizzly robe thudded so heavily across her arms that she staggered backward and stumbled over the fire-ring stones and fell on her tailbone. Laughter rang out around her. She collected the robe and limped with as much dignity as she could back to her bed.

But clutching the thick red-gold fur in her hands made her embarrassment fade, and after a moment, when Wolfstar appeared in the mouth of the tunnel, she allowed an almost friendly feeling to show in her face. He strode over, children chattering and jumping like crickets around him. The girl held the robe up and buried her face in fur, breathing in the bear scent.

Wolfstar spoke, and she lifted her head to see his hands. *Every time we pass the priest's lodge your eyes are searching for this,* he said. *So I talked him out of it.*

She said nothing, and he did not seem to want a reply. He sat on the bed robes beside her, tickling a shaven-headed toddler.

After a moment she spoke. He turned to her, laughing. *Why are you kind to me?* she formed hesitantly.

He thought about this, then replied, *That is my job.* Eyes sparkling, he added, *I also was afraid you might kill the priest in his sleep to get that robe.*

She did not know whether to be angry or to laugh. She pretended not to understand.

Though the days were hot, she took her grizzly robe everywhere. She was glad when Wolfstar drove the horses to pasture with the other boys, for then she could see Bull, and Wolfstar tolerated her tending the horse's saddle sores and brushing away the flies. The boys would herd the horses across the river in the morning, then lean back on the riverbank and talk, sometimes thoughtfully,

124

sometimes boisterously. She did her best to shut them out, but, forced to sit there with Wolfstar, she had nothing to do but watch his hands and listen. Gradually she began to understand more of their talk in spite of herself.

Wolfstar made many jokes; sometimes he joked about her and would look to see if she understood, but she pretended not to, though she did more and more. His words were beginning to penetrate to the same guarded place within her that Laughing Crow's words once had; but not like arrows, rather like threads of light. It gave her a strange feeling. She never spoke or joined in the laughter, or showed in any way that she understood their language.

But when Wolfstar challenged her to a horse race one morning she could not resist. *Around that willow and back. Choose any horse,* he offered. *I'll ride the little buckskin—she's the fastest in the village.*

The girl squinted at the willow far in the distance. *Then I choose her,* she signed, stifling a laugh. Wolfstar's friends laughed, too.

All right, he answered in good humor. *I will see how your big gelding runs.*

He untied her hands and fetched the horses. Stepping into a friend's hands, he climbed onto Bull's back and swung him around. Her palms dampened as she suddenly thought of fleeing.

Wolfstar nodded and she vaulted onto the buckskin and kicked hard. Wolfstar bolted after her, leaving the boys cheering behind them.

125

She approached the willow with a wide lead. To turn, or keep running? At the last instant, she pulled the mare up sharply, rounding the tree. She pounded up to the finish five lengths ahead.

Your gelding is slow, complained Wolfstar when he reached the heckling crowd. *You ride him.*

She willingly traded mounts, and they raced off again. This time she did not hesitate at the turn. The little mare was tired now, and Bull, making up in stamina what he lacked in speed, beat her.

You win, Wolfstar conceded with a smile as he slid from the buckskin's back. He wiped dust from his eyes. *You've proven what they say about Apsaalooka horsemanship. But is it not also true that your own legs are lazy from riding everywhere?*

Let us see, the girl replied with great pleasure, and, stepping beside him, coiled her muscles to sprint.

Wolfstar gave her an approving look. He leaned over and tensed beside her.

One of the boys started the race with a shout.

She ran across the long grass as hard as she could. Wolfstar trailed by a stride or two until after they had rounded the willow, then she could hear him gaining, until he surged past her. He burst past the cluster of boys far ahead.

She bent with her hands on her knees, panting, as the boys slapped Wolfstar on the back, laughing and shouting, setting up more races among themselves. After a moment she nudged Wolfstar and signed, *Once more.*

Wolfstar was still breathing so hard he could not speak, but he shook his head. He had lost something, he signed: a little yellow bag from his belt. He searched for the missing pouch until the sun was hot overhead, but he did not find it.

17

THE CORN WAS JUST HIGH ENOUGH TO BRUSH A
horse's belly the day the camp began the trek to the buffalo grounds. Dreamer was smeared from head to foot
with red grease-paint and pranced about on a horse with
eagle feathers braided into its mane and tail. From across
the crowd of travelers Hummingbird-in-her-hair met the
girl's eyes in a way that seemed to say goodbye.

The girl caught sight of the priest astride a paint pony,
trailing Bull behind him. It grieved her to escape the
Pawnee village without Bull, especially to leave him
among a people who honored horses so little. But she
had few choices.

Tears streamed down many faces as families parted.
Without warriors, the Stay-at-homes would be in grave
danger should enemies attack. But Her-corn-says-so em-
braced the members of her family one by one without
sign of fear or sorrow. Her homely face was quiet and

soft. From his horse, Two-voices laid a hand on the side of his wife's face and kissed her. Then he spoke to Wolfstar in his gritty and squeaking voices.

"Take care of your mother." He tossed his head toward the girl. "Take care of her," he said, and something else that she could not understand.

"Yes, Father," Wolfstar answered quietly. Two-voices clapped him on the shoulder.

She felt a pang in her chest, watching the old man's eyes as he looked at the boy. The pang stayed until long after Two-voices and the rest of the travelers had dipped behind a distant hill and were lost to sight.

Now the village was all but deserted, and the Stay-at-homes moved together into a single lodge for company and protection. The girl's bed was farthest from the entrance tunnel, and there would now be twice as many people to avoid disturbing when she crept out during the night, but as most were women and children, she was not concerned. She took her time in preparation for the night of her escape, hoarding bread and corn balls and pemmican in growing lumps under the buffalo robes of her bed.

Since Dreamer and his family had gone on the hunt, she ate all her meals in the communal lodge. Her walks with Wolfstar were strange now, with no one else about. His voice carved an oddly pleasing design through the empty village as he chattered at her, but though she understood more and more of his talk, she did not answer.

He seemed content to ramble on, as she had often done to Bull.

Two of Wolfstar's friends, whose names she had learned were Yellow-tail and Sticking-his-tongue-out, had also stayed home, and although there were few horses to guard now, all four of them often went to tend the animals. It was a much cooler and easier job than hauling water to the crops.

"I am bored with all this peace and quiet," Yellow-tail said one misty evening as they leaned back on the riverbank. "I wish the Comanche would attack and give me something to do."

"If only Pretty-elk-walking were still here," said Wolfstar with mock wistfulness, "there would not be so much boring peace and quiet. We would be listening to her yelling at you and to the sound of your courting flute breaking over your head." The three boys laughed.

Sticking-his-tongue-out was working a thin weed between his upper front teeth. "Pretty-elk-walking is good to look at, but I am more interested in a good cook," he said. "Two-voices' younger cousin."

Yellow-tail agreed that she was a wise choice. "What about you?" he asked Wolfstar. "You talk loud enough about my trying to court Pretty-elk-walking, but I don't see you having great luck with women."

Wolfstar looked as if Yellow-tail had punched the breath out of him. He said nothing, only pursed his lips. Yellow-tail's face turned ashen as he realized his indiscretion.

"Certainly he has," Sticking-his-tongue-out said. "Have you no eyes? The Morning Star girl follows him around like a buffalo calf," he teased. The girl wondered why he called her by this name. "What is she called again?"

Wolfstar smiled thinly, and all three boys were relieved at Sticking-his-tongue-out's quick thinking. "Danger-with-snarled-hair," Wolfstar said. The boys laughed as though this joke were new to them, and fell into an awkward lull.

"I am called," she said icily in Pawnee, "Grizzly-fears-her."

Wolfstar's companions were struck dumb. The girl's speech, though sharply accented, was unmistakably their own language. Their eyes darted to one another's faces in alarm.

"I hope you've been careful with your tongue," Yellow-tail snapped.

Sticking-his-tongue-out raised his eyebrows so high the whole bald crown of his head wrinkled.

It pleased the girl that she had disconcerted them. She was not truly satisfied with the name Grizzly-fears-her, but she could not wait forever. She rocked forward onto her feet and rose to leave. Wolfstar's hand shot toward her wrist, but recoiled short of touching it, as if he had suddenly remembered something. She strode away so they would not see the smile on her face.

Wolfstar did not follow—she could not go far. "A fitting name," she heard him say loudly. "That must be how she came by such a fine robe and necklace—she scared the bear to death. Imagine a poor grizzly stumbling upon such a wild-eyed, snarly-haired creature. I would have dropped dead of fright, too."

Wolfstar's companions burst into laughter. She tried to think of a scathing reply, but instead felt a laugh surfacing from deep within her.

"I have called you Danger-with-snarled-hair to your face many times," Wolfstar called after her. "Why do you correct me now?"

Yes, why did she correct him now? She did not know. Nor did she know why, when she rose that night without waking a soul, instead of escaping, she stole a buffalo tongue from Her-corn-says-so's things, crawled back under her covers, and secretly combed her hair.

18

THE MOON WHEN THE BERRIES TURN RED HAD
waned when she began to talk. The squash and bean
fields were like dark green lakes in the waist-high prairie
grass. The cornstalks had grown taller than a man, and
their pale yellow tassels fluttered in the wind as she and
Wolfstar walked and talked among the whispering plants.
The sun was burning hot, much hotter than it had ever
been in her valley. On the hottest days, they spent afternoons in the earthen lodge.

Wolfstar had grown used to his name for her, and kept
calling her Danger-with-snarled hair. In kind, she continued to call him Wolfstar.

"Wolfstar is not my name; I am merely keeper of the
Wolf Star bundle," he insisted one afternoon as they sat
in the lodge on her bed. He had been teaching her new
Pawnee words by carving their pictures into the floor
with his knife. Outside, the sky was white-hot, but in

the lodge it was dim and cool. Most of the Stay-at-homes were working or playing indoors. Her-corn-says-so and the other women sat with their backs against the tree trunks encircling the fire pit, chatting over mounds of dried corn they were grinding. The children squirmed restlessly on their grandmothers' laps.

"Do you know about sacred bundles?" Wolfstar asked.

"Yes, my people also have them," she said. "Sometimes we wear small ones about our necks as medicine."

"Ah, I had one of those," Wolfstar said wistfully, fingering where the small yellow buckskin bag had hung from his belt. "It held my own sacred objects. The Wolf Star bundle is much larger, and it belongs to our whole village, the Village-across-a-ridge. I am its keeper."

"As you are *my* keeper."

Wolfstar pursed his lips. "Yes," he admitted.

Silence hung between them for a time before he spoke again.

"The Wolf Star bundle is almost as old as the land," he said in a hushed voice. He turned to her with a strange intensity. "You see, the stars are very powerful—like gods. In the beginning of the universe, all the stars held a council." He carved a circle of crosses in the dirt, then a lone cross. "But they forgot to invite the Wolf Star. This angered him, and he became their enemy. When Paruksti, the storm god, carried human beings to earth in his whirlwind bag, the Wolf Star created a wolf to stalk him." From the boy's knife a storm god spiraled up in the dirt; then came a wolf, as he had drawn it that first night.

"While Paruksti slept, the wolf stole the bag of humans and let them out. The people set up camp and feasted the wolf on pemmican." Wolfstar illustrated each turn of the tale with deft strokes of his blade. "When Paruksti awoke and saw they were entertaining the intruder, he was angry. Realizing their mistake, the people chased and killed the wolf," he finished, stabbing the picture wolf.

Wolfstar wiped his knife on his breechcloth as though the dust were wolf's blood. "But the wolf's death did not satisfy Paruksti. Although the gods had meant human beings to live forever, Paruksti told them that now they must be visited by death. He made them dry the wolf's skin and make a sacred bundle with it. From that day they have been known as the Wolf People. These are my people."

The girl watched the wolf undulating in the firelight like a ghost.

"The sacred bundle was entrusted to one man, who handed it down to his son, and he to his son. This bundle has passed from father to son for a thousand lifetimes," Wolfstar said gravely. "Through wars, through famines, through sicknesses—the long line has never been broken. Now it has been handed from my father to me."

She looked at the boy beside her with new eyes. This

was no mere boy—a carefree, joking boy who could not even shoot straight.

She said quietly, "Two-voices adopted you because he had no son?"

"Yes. He had one son before me, but he was killed by Comanche." Wolfstar tapped the blade of his knife against the palm of his hand. "I was very nearly killed myself once," he said as though it surprised him. "When I was very small, in a raid. My father brought me to live here with the Wolf People, and nursed me back to health. Though he was not yet my father then; that is when he became my father." Wolfstar squinted at the reflections in his knife. "He sat by my bedside night and day until I was well, tending me with his own hands."

His words awakened the pang that had been sleeping in the girl's chest since the morning Wolfstar and his father had said goodbye.

"He must have wanted very much for you to live," she said.

"Yes. And I would lay down my life for him."

Suddenly a squealing little girl raced over the sleeping pallet and skidded behind Wolfstar, clutching his shirt.

"Save me! Save me!" she shrieked in delight as a pack of pursuing children piled into Wolfstar. He crushed the little warriors in a hug, growling like a bear and pretending to maul them. One by one they squirmed out of his grasp and threw themselves back on top of him with childish war whoops. Overcome with excitement, the little girl he was protecting tackled him, too.

"Look!" Wolfstar said, shaking one of the boys by the scruff of his shirt. "How did a Lakota raider sneak right into the middle of camp?" Wolfstar sent the boy off with a spank and instantly the children stampeded after him.

"Well, then, your name is not Wolfstar," the girl allowed after a moment. "But of course I do not need to know your name, anyway, since the Pawnee refer to each other by kin terms."

Wolfstar smiled uncomfortably and seemed to shake his head.

"You told me yourself—the people do not call Hercorn-says-so by her name but mother or aunt or sister, remember?" she said. "So, how should I address you? Brother?"

"Son!" Her-corn-says-so shrilled across the lodge. "I have told you a hundred times not to stir up the children inside. Now look at this mess."

Rising more quickly than most boys would rise to such a call, Wolfstar looked down and said, "Call me Wolfstar, then, if it pleases you," and strode away to clean up the cornmeal.

They spent cooler days on the trail from the river to the fields, hauling water to the crops, or hunting for breadroot or other foods for the women to prepare. Wolfstar never required or even asked the girl to help with the chores, even those which she thought unsuitable work for a man, especially a man of Wolfstar's stature. After the work was done, or sometimes before, they joined

Wolfstar's friends for a swim in the river or a shooting match.

Evenings after supper, Wolfstar was always careful to retie her hands; then they climbed to the top of the high ridge above the village, where he took up his post as sentinel. There they would sit together and talk. Often Wolfstar sang, to let the enemy know someone was watching, and, depending on the winds, they sometimes heard other sentinels talking or singing in the distance. As the stars appeared, Wolfstar would tell her about them.

"See that fiery star?" Wolfstar cried one evening at dusk. "Over there—the Spirit Star. You don't often see him glowing like that."

They watched it burn low on the horizon for an instant, then disappear.

"That is a bad omen," Wolfstar said somberly. "When the Spirit Star rises thus, it means that a great person will soon die."

Reminded of what Sticking-his-tongue-out had called her, she asked, "Why did your friend call me the Morning Star girl?"

Wolfstar hesitated. "We believe everyone is under the guidance of a certain star."

After thinking awhile, she said, "I do not think I believe in your star gods."

"Hmm," Wolfstar said absently. "What do you believe in?"

"In dreams," she said, not certain she should reveal

this. Though she was not cold, she pulled her grizzly robe close about her shoulders. She did not look at Wolfstar but at a weed sticking up between her moccasins. "I believe in one certain dream. My father dreamed it before I was born."

Out of the corner of her eye she saw that Wolfstar was watching her intently. "He dreamed that I would be special," she ventured, not daring to say the full truth.

Wolfstar smiled his crooked smile. "He was right."

She felt as if a sun were burning in her. Her palms were sweating. Finally she said, "The dream said that I would number among the greatest Apsaalooka ever to live."

Wolfstar was not smiling now. She could feel respect in his gaze, and something else as well.

"We, too, believe in dreams," he said.

A long, uncomfortable silence fell over them.

"Why is Dreamer called Dreamer instead of a kin word?" the girl asked.

"That is a long story," Wolfstar said.

"Tell it to me."

Wolfstar drilled into the dirt with his knife. "He had a dream that we consider very important," he said at last.

His hesitant manner sharpened her curiosity. "What dream?"

"Oh, it has to do with our people and the stars—too difficult to explain," he said, and began to sing. *"Tsasiri pirus, he, witi-tirak-tap-pirihuru,"* he intoned in a clear voice that rang over the plains.

"You are always singing that," she said. "What kind of Pawnee nonsense is it: 'Even worms, each other they-them-love'?"

Wolfstar looked at her as though she were a small child requiring much patience. "It is far from nonsense. It means, all creatures need love. It is in their nature. Even worms love each other."

She turned this over in her mind. "So?"

"So," Wolfstar said, "you may as well not fight it." He shook his head and laughed at her. "Why are you so contrary? Can't anything just be? Maybe you should stop thinking so hard for once and just be. Why not sing with me? *Tsasiri pirus, he* . . . Come on . . . *witi-tirak-tap-pirihuru.*"

"It is too foolish."

"*Tsasiri pirus, he,*" he sang louder, urging her to join in. "I am not going to stop until you sing with me."

She resisted, pressing her lips tightly together to keep from smiling.

Wolfstar kept singing. Finally he stood up and began dancing. He marched with his knees high, now tossing his head back, now dropping it down on his chest. He reminded her of her own people's Horse Dance. Even his thin strip of hair looked like the special headdress the Apsaalooka warriors wore during the dance to imitate a horse's mane.

"Even worms, even worms," he sang, and paused to make a face at her.

She burst out laughing.

"Even worms," he whispered, beckoning with a tiny motion of his hands.

"Each other they-them-love," she said crossly.

"Come on, louder."

"Even worms, each other they-them-love," she shouted, trying not to like it.

"*Sing* it," he said, tugging at her sleeve to stand up. She sang as foolishly as she could.

"That's it!" Wolfstar whooped as she scrambled to her feet and began mimicking his dance. "*Tsasiri pirus, he, witi-tirak-tap-pirihuru,*" they sang over and over at the top of their lungs. Raising her knees was awkward with her hands tied, and she finally lost her balance and collapsed onto the ground.

"Now will you stop singing that song," she gasped. "My ears are sick of it!"

A faint voice down by the river called, "So are all our ears!"

The two looked at each other mischievously. "Even worms," they howled simultaneously, and collapsed in laughter.

The last protests echoed between the lodges, and their laughter faded. A crescent moon was beginning to rise. Along the horizon where the sun had sunk out of sight was only a pale green glow. In the turquoise above, the Evening Star and her few companions burned.

"This is my favorite time of day," the girl ventured softly.

In the waning light, Wolfstar turned and studied her.

She had let the big robe slip from her shoulders, and the breeze brushed her long hair in black swirls across the blond fur. Two strands of hair had tangled in the fingerlike ivory claws of the necklace, which was so large that it covered her chest. He glanced at her scarred hands.

"Danger," he asked, "did you kill that bear?"

In her mind she could see again the golden beast lying still, staring at her lifelessly. "Yes," she said, not wishing to talk about this.

"How did you do it?" Wolfstar asked.

"With a knife."

It was not a very satisfying explanation. "I don't believe it," he said under his breath.

"I am no liar," she spat, stung by his words.

"No," Wolfstar said in distress. "I meant—" He leaned toward her and came so close to setting his arm around her shoulders that she could feel its heat, but then withdrew. "I know you are not a liar."

He began to sing again, quietly, a different song this time.

She looped her arms over her knees and hugged them close to her chest.

After a time, Wolfstar turned toward her again. He slid his knife out of its sheath and cut through the lashing between her wrists. Then he replaced the knife, sat back, and began to sing again.

She looked at him sideways through her hair. "How do

you know I will not turn on you now and kill you and flee?" she asked.

Wolfstar's eyes danced. "Because half a moon ago I cleaned your store of corn bread from your bedcovers and fed it to the dogs, and you have not even missed it."

In spite of the blow to her pride, she laughed. "How dare you throw my bread to the dogs?"

"It was rancid. Fried bread doesn't keep forever," he said, shaking his head. "You have much to learn about our ways."

"Well, then, I will simply steal some pemmican from your mother's storage pit when I escape tonight," she said, crossing her arms.

Wolfstar did not remind her that she had claimed she was no liar.

She squinted into the stars, still feeling the warmth from Wolfstar's arm. She did not think.

19

THE PRAIRIE SKY WAS ENORMOUS. THE ENDLESS sprawling grassland seemed small and contained in comparison with the sky arching overhead. Wisps of cloud clung to its ceiling, while thicker clumps of cloud drifted so low that in the distance they seemed to be resting on the hills.

The girl sat cross-legged on the baked earth with her hands in her lap. Her gaze floated down from the sky to the grass, grayish from the hot, dry summer, but warmed to gold now by the late afternoon sun.

Wolfstar was leaning back on his elbows nearby. These hot, slow days of quiet talk and silences that were like a kind of talk, too, were nearly over. The moon-when-the-leaves-turn-yellow was coming, and the village would soon return. But on days like this it was as if no other season existed but summer with Wolfstar.

"I feel as if I could almost reach up and touch those

clouds," he said. He lay down and stretched his arms above his head. "I have always wondered what they feel like."

She brushed a biting ant off her leg. "They feel cold and wet," she said. "You would not miss much if you never touch one."

"Have you touched a cloud?" he asked incredulously, sitting up and twisting to face her.

"I walked right through it. It was like fog."

"You honestly touched a cloud?"

"It is not so difficult," she said irritably. She was trying to console him, since in this low-lying country he would never come close to a cloud. Wolfstar was staring at her as if she were a spirit.

"You must climb a mountain," she added, since he kept staring. "Mountains often reach into the clouds."

"I would like to climb a mountain," he said, trying to recover himself. "I have never even seen one."

"Someday you can travel to my country; there you can climb as many as you like."

Wolfstar sighed. "I don't think so . . ."

"Something else you should see, on the way to my country," she said. "Once in your life you should visit the Land of Boiling Waters." She told him about the steaming holes in the ground, the black cliff, the yellow-canyon waterfall, the burbling pools. The one thing she did not tell him was how she loved the colors, how they made her feel like singing.

Wolfstar was absorbed in her telling of the place. "That I would like to see with my own eyes," he almost whispered. "You have been so many places. I have never been outside my own village."

"But you could go."

"I cannot go far." He let himself fall back into the grass. "I cannot even marry outside my village," he said in the voice usually reserved for Dreamer.

He seemed to be thinking of a certain girl—an outsider—whom he wanted to marry.

"If I did marry outside the Village-across-a-ridge, we would lose the Wolf Star bundle, for then it would belong to *her* village," he said.

The girl looked over at him, but he was hidden in the long grass. "Who would you want to marry from outside your village?" she asked.

He waited a long time before answering. Quietly he said, "I wanted to marry Hummingbird-in-her-hair. And she wanted to marry me."

"Oh," the girl said, feeling like a stone. "Why is she with Dreamer?"

"We could never wed," Wolfstar said. "She is from the Village-in-the-bottomlands." He began tearing a weed into small pieces. "Anyway, I had nothing to offer. She needed someone older, useful to her family, to protect them and provide for them. Girls always marry someone older. That is the way of things."

She crawled over to Wolfstar and crushed down the

grass near his head so she could see him. "You could have married her anyway," she said.

"That was long ago," he said, sounding tired. "And it is not that simple. Our lives are not really our own. You of all people should understand that. The gods wanted you to become great among your people. That is your path. We must all follow the path given us. Mine is to be the Wolf Star bundle keeper."

"You know nothing," she said. "Do you think my path was handed to me, just like that? No. I had to fight for it—with all my strength, from the instant I was born. They all thought my twin brother was the Great One, and I was nothing. Even my own father. I grew up like an orphan."

Confusion clouded Wolfstar's face.

"I worked hard," she murmured. "By the time I was eight winters old I could shoot three arrows through a hoop before it fell. That was when my father finally believed. I said to him, 'Look at me! My brother is dead. I have survived. Have you ever thought that *I* am the one?' But no one else believed."

Wolfstar stared at her.

"I know, you are thinking I am bad in the head. I am used to that," she said and laughed hollowly. "Everyone in my village thinks I am bad in the head, like my father. Even *I* didn't believe myself, until this." She shook her bear-claw necklace. "You see this? And this robe? They are all I have to prove that I am not no one—that I am the Great One.

"Now you know the truth," she said bitterly. "I did not want you to." The wind kicked her hair up in her face, and she did not brush it aside. "I tell you so you will see that you do not have to lie down and die simply because your village expects you to. Even if your own father expects you to."

After a long moment, he said, "I see. But if I refuse to do what is asked of me, my people will perish."

She was stunned. How could it be—that this boy should be responsible for his whole people?

Finally she shook her head. "I do not understand any god that asks you to go against your heart," she said.

"Nor do I," Wolfstar said in less than a whisper.

The corn was twice her height and "in the milk," as Wolfstar called it. It would soon be ready for harvest. The squash and pumpkins glowed in yellows and oranges, and some of the beans were bursting their pods.

Wolfstar was pouring his last skin of water on a row of pony-spotted beans. "The rest of the village will be home from the hunt soon," he announced, and tossed the empty waterskins and pole aside on the dirt.

The girl was not certain how she felt about this news. She looked forward to the return of excitement and games, but she did not want to give up the quiet summer she had shared with Wolfstar. The fondness she felt for Hummingbird-in-her-hair had changed to confusion. She did not like to think of Wolfstar loving

Hummingbird-in-her-hair, even if it was in the past, though she told herself she did not care.

"We will not have many more times," Wolfstar continued, "alone together." Looking around furtively, he beckoned her into the sunflowers. "I want to give you this, before the others return." Uncertainly, she followed.

Wolfstar held out a fist and opened his fingers.

In his palm lay a small, narrow arrowhead, crudely cut of bright blue stone marbled with shades of green. A thin strip of pale orange metal had been coiled around the stem and curled up from it in a hook.

"It's an ear pendant, since you already have a necklace," he said shyly. "I worked on it while you were shooting with the boys. It's your colors. See, the colors of your favorite time of day?"

She tried to say something, but all she could do was bite her lip. She was afraid to reach for the gift.

"I know your ears are not pierced, but that's easy to do. I would have made two, but I only had stone enough for one."

Pressing down a powerful urge to run away, she nodded.

Wolfstar walked over to the field and peeled the silk back from an ear of corn and broke off the tip of the cob. "Don't worry, I've seen this done many times," he said, slipping a bone needle from a flat pouch. "Which ear?"

Raising both hands nervously to her throat, she touched a finger to her left ear.

Her hair was covering the ear, and as she began to brush it away, Wolfstar lifted the thick strand and smoothed it back. She felt the moist corncob behind her earlobe, the heat of his hands, then the sting of the needle, and the thread of blood dribbling down the side of her throat. Most acutely of all, she felt the absence of his touch.

He slipped the hook into her earlobe and twisted the wire around itself. With a bit of cornhusk he whisked the blood off her neck.

"Just keep the wound packed with grease for a few days and it will heal." He stood back to look at her.

"You should not—I cannot—" she stammered.

Abruptly he turned and walked toward the village.

She stood trying to keep her balance; was it the sunflowers swaying or herself?

"Wait!" she called after him, and raced down the path. "What am I to you, Wolfstar? Please don't joke with me now," she pleaded as she caught up to him. "A sister? What? I must know." She reached toward him and he shrank back in alarm.

Very slowly, Wolfstar said, "I am sorry. I can't explain. I can't—"

"Am I so horrible that you can't stand the thought of touching me?" she cried.

"Don't be foolish," he said fiercely, grasping her arms through her calfskin dress. "I have responsibilities." Wolfstar flung her arms down. He rubbed his hands over his head as if trying to hold it together.

150

"I can't explain," he said quietly. "Please do not ask me to."

He strode away. This time she let him go.

That evening they trudged up the long hill to their sentinel post in silence. The sun was still burning red atop the horizon. The girl sat on her feet, trying to summon the courage to speak the words she had been practicing in her mind.

"Wolfstar," she said finally, too loudly, "I have something I want to give you, also."

Wolfstar looked at her, puzzled, perhaps wondering what she possibly had to give.

She slipped her hands under her hair and unlooped the leather clasp of her bear-claw necklace.

"No, I couldn't take that!" Wolfstar exclaimed.

"I want you to," she said, holding it out with trembling hands, as she would offer a sacred pipe.

"I can't. This necklace means too much to you."

"That is why I want to give it to you," she said. "Don't worry—I will still have my robe."

Wolfstar shook his head. "There is so much you don't know . . ."

"I know enough. I know that your star gods have commanded you to go against your heart," she said. She dared to look into his eyes. "But they cannot command me to go against mine."

Wolfstar looked away. "As you wish," he said heavily.

She stood and walked behind him. Then she draped

the heavy necklace over his chest. Her stiff and nervous hands needed several attempts to hook the clasp. She walked around and sat beside him. He had only needed a necklace; he was a fine-looking young man.

"It feels as though it's yet glowing with the grizzly's spirit," he said, touching the thick fur reverently. "Or yours. Your spirits are much the same." He breathed in deeply. "I will remember you by this, Danger-with-snarled-hair."

She looked out at the evening sky darkening to her favorite time of day. From this day on, the green and blue would no longer be simply her favorite colors, but also the colors of Wolfstar's gift to her.

She did not say that she was certain he would not need to remember her, that in the end his heart must win out over the stars. She merely began singing, "Even worms . . ."

20

THOUGH SHE WAS TARGET-SHOOTING FOR ARROWS
down in the bottomlands, she saw the movements from
a long way off. They were the movements of people on
horseback, heavily laden and dragging travois.

"The village is coming," she exclaimed, and ran toward
the lodges. Sticking-his-tongue-out and Yellow-tail came
running after her.

They reached the lodges just as three scouts were galloping in.

"Was the hunt successful?" shouted Yellow-tail.

The scouts' victorious shrills answered plainly. They
wheeled their horses around in front of the communal
lodge and began tossing packets of meat to the women
gathering in the doorway. The Stay-at-homes crowded
around to hear the news.

"The buffalo were so thick, we could hardly get among
them to hunt," one of the scouts called out with a laugh.

"What of our men?" asked Her-corn-says-so.

"Your husband is well," the scout said. "Three men injured, but none were lost. We did lose many horses."

"Which horses?" the girl wanted to know. "What about the big black-and-gold gelding?" The scouts seemed taken aback at her speaking to them in their own tongue, but they had no response, for none had given a thought to individual horses.

Wolfstar pushed through the crowd. "Did Dreamer take a fat cow?" he asked, but his voice was drowned in the clamor as the rest of the party began pouring over the ridge.

Dreamer led the way on foot, trailing his horse behind him. On its back was strapped a slaughtered buffalo cow, feet upward.

She pointed it out to Wolfstar. "Is it important?"

"It's important to a ceremony we will soon hold," he said, squinting.

"Then it's good that he took the cow."

"I don't know," Wolfstar said vaguely, as if he had forgotten the question. He rushed on to meet his father.

The girl caught sight of Hummingbird-in-her-hair in the crowd, and lifted her hand shyly, but the Pawnee girl did not see her.

The Stay-at-homes ran up the hillside, darting among the swarms of horses and travois and people and yapping dogs, searching for their loved ones. She ran with them, nearly colliding with the priest astride his buffalo pony. Tied behind, Bull labored under several large rawhide packets of buffalo meat. She raced to him and rubbed his broad face and laughed as he snorted and tried to nip her.

"Bull, you big puppy," she said in Apsaalooka, "I'm so glad to see you. Are you all right? You are covered with dust! Did they treat you well?"

Bull sneezed in response. She tried to pry up his burden to check his back for raw spots.

"Get back from there!" called the priest, twisting around in his saddle.

"I will see you at pasture, Bull," she said into the horse's neck, and with an affectionate slap she ran on.

She spotted Two-voices on top of the rise, sliding off his horse into the arms of Her-corn-says-so. He threw his arms around his wife and clasped her against him. They were still standing there holding each other when the girl arrived, just behind Wolfstar.

"My son," Two-voices said with mostly his squeaking voice. He reached a hand behind Wolfstar's head and pulled the boy to his chest.

"Father," Wolfstar said quietly. "Dreamer killed a fat cow."

"Yes," Two-voices said, and released his grip on Wolfstar to look into his eyes. Wolfstar looked away, chewing on his lip. Two-voices put an arm around him and, with his other arm around Her-corn-says-so, clucked at the horse, and they all started down the hill.

"I see you have taken care of the girl. And your mother," Two-voices said. He squeezed his wife closer to him. "I trust you have also taken care of the fields. How are the crops?"

"Quite good," Wolfstar said.

"Oh, they are looking wonderful," the girl chimed in, walking alongside. "Almost everyone's corn is in the milk, and most of the flat beans are ready for picking. The sun shone hot here nearly every day you were gone, and Wolf-star brought water—" She stopped speaking as she realized she was alone. She turned to look back and saw Two-voices standing on the hillside, clutching his son's and wife's shoulders, glaring.

"What goes on here in my absence?" he demanded.

Her-corn-says-so said softly, "It's all right, old man." But her face looked anxious.

"She is quick with our language," Wolfstar said. "She could not help picking it up."

"She is carrying a bow," Two-voices snapped. "And a quiverful of arrows."

"She has not run away," Wolfstar said disrespectfully. "She might have run away many times, but she hasn't."

"This is true," Her-corn-says-so agreed.

Two-voices was scowling.

The girl looked from one family member to another, and finally, her eyes meeting the old man's, she said earnestly, "I want to stay."

Two-voices grunted his disapproval.

"It's all right, old man," Her-corn-says-so said again, and pressed him to walk on. He allowed her to lead him down the hill to the lodge, but the matter seemed far from settled.

She had never seen such abundance. All along the hillside, women scraped at buffalo hides stretched out on pegs. One could barely walk between all the drying racks sagging with buffalo strips and pumpkin rings, and the beans spread underfoot. Popping noises filled the air as the beans dried in the sun. The mouth-watering aroma of new corn roasting wafted across the prairie from dozens of pits dotting the countryside.

Since the return of the buffalo hunters, Wolfstar seemed under great strain. Two-voices did not hide his disapproval of his son's treatment of their Apsaalooka captive, and although he did not interfere, he and Wolfstar hardly spoke to each other. When the girl talked to Wolfstar, he seemed far away. He had important things on his mind, he said, preparing for his responsibilities in the ceremony.

The day of the ceremony, the Morning Star rose with a red ring around it. At their meal of tiny boiled pumpkins everyone was tense. There was none of the usual joking. Her-corn-says-so did not speak a word, and the silence between Wolfstar and Two-voices was like screaming.

"Perhaps you should try to speak to your father about

me," the girl suggested to Wolfstar later as they spread out with a group of boys and men hunting for wood to stoke the roasting fires.

Wolfstar was constantly squinting, though the sun was hidden behind a cloud bank. As they combed the tall grass he would pick up a stick of wood, and then a few steps later absently toss it away. "What could I say," he murmured.

She avoided looking at him. "You could tell him that I don't have a real home in my own village. This could be my village now."

Wolfstar nodded, but he seemed not to be listening.

"So you wouldn't have to lose the Wolf Star bundle to another village," she explained. "And I have no family to provide for."

He turned toward her, blinking. "What?"

"And I'd work, I'd work hard. I'm a good hunter. But I could learn women's work if you want me to."

"Stop," Wolfstar said angrily. "Stop talking that way."

She stepped toward him. "But—you do care for me?"

"What does it matter?" He plucked a branch from where it leaned against a yucca plant.

"Wolfstar, you have picked that stick up three times. What's wrong with you?"

He flung the branch away. "I need to be alone," he snapped.

Angrily, she stalked off. She would go visit Bull. Surely Wolfstar did care for her, but he seemed to have more responsibilities than she knew. She wondered if there was truly no answer to this problem. She picked a few stray cobs of sweet corn along the path to the river. The water was so low from the hot summer that by leaping from one sandbar to another she crossed without wetting her feet. She crouched to scoop mud from the riverbed into her skirt, and called a greeting to the string of boys sitting on the other bank, watching the horses, but strangely, they only stared at her. She shrugged off their rudeness and walked out onto the plain where the horses were grazing.

While Bull munched at the corncobs, she soothed his saddle sores with mud and complained to him about Wolfstar. She spent the whole morning and much of the afternoon among the horses, packing up the raw spots on every one that would let her near.

"That will keep the flies off," she said to a paint mare, wiping the last of the mud off her hands onto the long grass. A leather thong trailing from under the mare's hoof caught her eye. It ran to a little yellow buckskin bag. Wolfstar's medicine bundle, she realized, and pushed the mare's foreleg off it.

She splashed through the river and walked up the foot-path toward the village. Almost everyone was outside, shucking corn or tanning hides or gathering wood. They stopped talking and averted their eyes as she passed. Her cheeks burned. Did the whole village know, then, how she had thrown herself at Wolfstar?

Of Wolfstar there was no sign. He must be inside. She walked around to the back of their lodge. She swung a leg up to the edge of the roof, hoisted herself up, and clambered to the top of the dome. Just as she was about to call to him down the smoke hole, she heard Two-voices saying, "A boy of your age cannot help feeling—I should not have placed such a responsibility on you. I pray you have not touched her."

She jerked her head back from the opening and flattened herself against the dirt. She knew these words were not meant for her ears, but she could not turn away.

"I have not," said Wolfstar.

"If you *have* touched her, I cannot save you," Two-voices said severely. "If the Morning Star decides to take you instead, there is nothing anyone can do."

"I have not touched her, Father," Wolfstar insisted.

"My son, it hurts me not to trust you."

"I gave up Hummingbird-in-her-hair," Wolfstar said coldly. "What more proof of my allegiance do you require?"

"I am warning you," Two-voices said in a way that sliced up the girl's spine. "Do not try anything foolish. She *will* be at the ceremony tonight. I know how painful it is for you. None of us *wants* to do it, but we must! Remember your people. The Morning Star must have the blood of that girl's heart, no matter what feelings you have for her."

Over the pounding in her ears, she heard Wolfstar

scoff, "Feelings for her? What feelings? I have done only what you taught me: be kind to her, keep her happy and ignorant of her fate so that she may be led through the ceremony willingly when the time comes. I think I have done my task well." His voice rang angrily through the lodge's rafters. "Yet you suggest I have betrayed you, betrayed my people!"

There was a long silence, broken only by the old man's sigh.

"Son . . ."

"Father, she will be at the ceremony tonight," Wolfstar said in a tender voice.

She was nearly sliding off the roof, but she did not care. Nothing mattered. Her heart had already been ripped from her breast.

21

THERE WAS ONLY DARKNESS IN HER NOW. HER old friend anger, who had led the fight to survive so many times before, guided her footsteps hurriedly away from the lodge. She must not be seen there; she must not raise any suspicion that she had overheard. Hastily she struggled to weigh her situation. There was no time to worry about food or even weapons. She had the clothes she was wearing, and she had freedom enough to go to the horses—no one would worry at seeing her among them. If she could linger in the pasture until dusk, she might not be seen slipping away. If only the ceremony did not begin before then! The sky was now gray as slate, so there would be no light tonight to follow her by. But what of her grizzly robe? She no longer took it everywhere, and this morning she had left it inside the lodge.

Aching, she looked back at the earthen dome. If she went back in the heat of the afternoon to fetch her robe, they would know something was amiss. And she could not face Wolfstar without revealing herself.

With tremendous effort she turned down the path to the river. As she strode along, she felt the ear pendant swinging against the side of her throat and ached to rip it out. But she did not dare, not until she was out of sight.

"Danger," Wolfstar called from the head of the path. She started violently and was afraid she had given herself away, but he was too far from her to notice. He trotted down to her, a loaded saddlebag bouncing from his shoulder and another large pack dragging behind him.

"I want to apologize for the way I acted earlier," he said. "You were right. I have been a coward. I won't be any longer." He adjusted his grip on his burdens, clenching them so that his knuckles whitened. "I will speak to my father tonight, after the ceremony."

His voice sounded so warm and safe, as always. Yes, he had done his task well. She clutched her wrist to stop herself from trying to crush his throat.

"Please don't be angry with me," Wolfstar said. "I am sorry."

She could not bear to see the necklace she had given him draped over his black-and-green-beaded ceremonial shirt.

"Here," she said abruptly, holding out his medicine bag. "Look what I found."

"Oh!" He seemed stunned, and looked up with real gratitude. "Thank you," he said quietly.

"It's all right, old man," she forced out, parodying Her-corn-says-so.

Briefly Wolfstar's lips parted in an unreal smile. "You are wanted in the lodge," he said. "My mother and my aunt have grown more corn than they can shuck."

She swallowed hard. She had never before been asked to work; they must want to keep her under watch until the ceremony. "I was going out to take care of the horses," she said as evenly as she could.

"My father has just sent me to see about one of his horses. I'll look after the others, too."

"I don't think . . ."

Wolfstar smiled knowingly. "Don't worry. I'll take good care of Bull for you."

"No—" she said, groping. When Wolfstar reached the pasture he would see the mud already on their backs and know she had lied. "You don't have to," she said. "I already plastered them up earlier; I just wanted to see . . . Sometimes the mud cracks off."

"You certainly care a lot about those beasts," Wolfstar said. "I'll tend them for you."

There was nothing to do but walk back up the path, with Wolfstar watching her, and go to help the women with their corn.

As she tore off husk after blackened husk from the roasted ears, and then joined in cutting the kernels off the cobs row by row, time seemed to drag endlessly, yet race. It seemed the moment would never come when she could escape. Yet the moment of her death was hurtling toward her as if she were falling off a cliff.

The lodge grew ominously dark, but whether from the oncoming dusk or a gathering storm she could not judge. She thought she heard thunder in the distance. Two-voices sat on his bed against the wall, where in the dim light she could barely see him; but she knew he was watching her.

After repeating the words over and over in her head until she thought she could say them naturally, she asked, "How much longer until the ceremony?"

A shadow crossed every face in the circle, and suddenly she realized that she was the only person in the village who had not known all along that she was to be sacrificed.

"Not long," Her-corn-says-so said without a hint of her feelings.

Wolfstar appeared in the passageway.

Her-corn-says-so laid her clamshell blade on the earthen floor. "Now," she said.

A raindrop blew against her face as they walked toward Dreamer's lodge, and at her feet more drops began splashing into the dust. Under the calfskin dress her body was slick with sweat. In desperation, she tried to walk slowly. Wolfstar walked on her left, Two-voices on her right, and the rest of the family behind her. Ahead, the whole village was gathering outside Dreamer's lodge. All the men and boys, even toddlers, carried bow and quiver. Many people had climbed onto the dome's roof and were ripping up the sod so they could watch through holes.

The horses had been driven into the village against the impending storm, and on the edge of the herd milled the swift little buckskin no more than twenty paces from her grasp. But though over that short distance she might outrace the Pawnee, she could never outrace their arrows.

The entrance tunnel gaped before her. Inside the lodge a fire burned, and at the end of the passageway stood the priest, his false smile seeming to welcome her.

Her only chance was to convince them she knew nothing, to submit to the ceremony and watch for an opportunity to escape.

She stepped into the tunnel.

22

THE FACES OF THE PRIEST, DREAMER, AND SEV-
eral assistants glowed red in the light of the embers, and
their long shadows writhed over the dome's walls above
the heads of the seated figures filling the lodge. Dimly lit
faces watched through jagged holes in the roof, and a
dozen more crowded the smoke hole, deathly somber.
There was no sound but the whisper of the fire and the
groan of faraway thunder.

Wolfstar bade her sit down on one of two buckskin
cushions near the fire pit, and sat beside her on the other.
Most of the remaining villagers squeezed in behind them
on the floor, stepping over four carefully laid out circles
of tiny breathfeathers. Between the feather circles lay
four long poles, longer than lodgepoles, pointing from
the fire like rays from the sun, to each of the four sacred
directions.

Shaking a gourd rattle, the priest began to sing mournfully. It was a simple but long song repeating over and

over that Mother Corn was in the lodge. On and on he sang, but after a time the girl no longer heard him. She must be calm. She must wait for an opening. Then she must run as she had never run in her life.

The priest finished his song, then sang more strange, repetitive songs that made no sense to her, though she understood the words. Between songs she could hear a heavy rain falling outside, although the roof deadened its roar to a sigh. As the slow-burning ends of the poles were gradually consumed, hands shoved the saplings farther into the fire. She watched the poles shrink, wondering if they measured how long she had left to live. Her thoughts began to blur as the songs droned on, and her muscles ached from the tension.

Dreamer marched to one of the poles jutting from the fire, knocked the coals off, and lifted its glowing point into the air. He wore striped leggings and an otter belt thickly tasseled with scalps, and his face and naked upper body had been washed with white, making him look like a spirit of the dead.

The priest began to sing, urgently now. "Oh, this is what I did: I became like him. I became ferocious, I became like him . . ."

Dreamer lurched forward into a frenetic dance. He stomped and wheeled with the pole in his hands, twisting it over his head and around his body. The red-hot point burst into flame and painted an orange trail in the darkness. Suddenly he stabbed the fiery point at the girl, so rapidly that she cried out before she realized she had not been touched. Again Dreamer whirled around and jabbed at her without striking.

"The earth; I became like him, I became ferocious," the priest chanted as Dreamer reeled through the lodge, sweeping up the other poles one by one from the fire and into his dance. He stomped out the feather circles, blasting white down into the air like a snowstorm. Her head was whirling as wildly as the dance. In the darkness the people's eyes gleamed red. With every lunge of the burning lance they shouted.

Abruptly the priest stopped singing. Dreamer laid the last pole, now no longer than a lance, into the fire once more and stepped back. Except for the heaving of his chest, he stood as still as the tree trunk pillars beside him. Sweat rinsed dark streaks through his white stain. The priest motioned to one of his assistants, who gathered a few coals from the fire and heaped them between the fire pit and the entrance tunnel. Kneeling beside them, he deftly cut a shock of sweet grass into bits and blended them into a lump of buffalo fat. He worked in silence, all eyes upon his hands.

How long she had been inside this lodge! The night must be nearly over. She looked up to the holes in the roof, still crowded with villagers, who were dripping but heedless of the storm. The rain-darkened fragments of sky that showed between them were of no use in distinguishing night from morning.

All these people around her, normally so spirited and free-spoken, were somber. Wolfstar sat like a stranger beside her. The weight of it all pressed upon her like the close air of those burning summer afternoons that now seemed from another lifetime.

The assistant set his mixture of sweet grass and fat on the coals. It sizzled and coughed up a cloud of smoke. The smoke rose and spread throughout the lodge, like the bad feeling that hung in the air and grew heavier with every passing moment.

Finally the priest turned to Wolfstar and spoke. "Bring the girl."

She did not move. Wolfstar stood over her, motioning for her to stand. All eyes were on her. Unable to think of any other course, she rose on trembling legs, and followed Wolfstar to the priest.

Dreamer stepped forward and drew up something in his hand that was visible only for the instant that the dim red glinted off it—a knife.

Her heartbeat crashed crazily through her body. As he raised the blade, her throat clenched tight as a fist. He began to slice, but she felt nothing. The blade did not touch her skin. Meticulously he slit only the calfskin dress, from collar to hem. The priest slipped the dress from her shoulders, and with hide daubers the assistants fell to painting her from head to ankle, black on one side and red on the other.

In her relief that Dreamer had not cut out her heart,

she barely felt the grease-paint being smeared on her body. How much longer could she keep this secret that everyone knew? At the edge of the fire pit she could barely make out one of the poles lying with one end in the fire—it was shorter than her arm.

The men had finished painting her. They slipped a new calfskin dress, black as her hair, over her head, and began chanting, "They are making you, they are making you, of earth."

This she understood: they were turning her back into earth: killing her. She could not control her trembling as they slid a pair of black moccasins onto her feet. The smoke and the fear and the heat from so many bodies made her grease-paint coating unbearable.

"They are making you, they are making you, of earth."

Opening a large hide box that must have been the Morning Star sacred bundle, the priest pulled out a bow and passed it four times through the smoke still rising from the sweet grass–buffalo fat ball. Then he reached for a quiver and performed the same ritual. Then an arrow, a red-bowled pipe, an ear of corn, owl skins. Four times each he guided the procession of sacred objects through the purifying smoke.

Lastly he fished out a long, braided leather cord. It, too, passed through the smoke four times before the priest reached out with it toward the girl's left hand, singing, "Cloud comes yonder. The thongs that are tied on. See, cloud comes yonder."

She strangled a scream as the priest began to tie her hands.

The thong tightened around her wrists as if around her throat. "Not for long does she look about, not for long does she stand," the priest cried as he lashed her hands. Tears trickled down his face, but the ever-present false smile twisted his expression into a grotesque leer.

Panic burbled up like bile in her throat. This must be the end.

Other voices joined in his song, many of the people weeping openly as they chanted, "Not for long does she stand, not for long does she move." Even Dreamer seemed mournful. Strangely, everyone grieved at killing her.

Everyone but Wolfstar. He stood nearby, dry-eyed.

Tears of horror swelled in her eyes. She continued to try to feign ignorance, though she was the only one still pretending. She felt the priest's hand on her shoulder like a spider. He gestured toward the smoke.

Slowly, she walked through it, her eyes stinging, her quiet movement belying her mounting hysteria.

He is afraid to touch me, she suddenly realized. Just like Wolfstar—they are all afraid the Morning Star will kill them if they touch me! Frantically, she grasped at this knowledge as the priest bade her walk through a second time. Not one of the Pawnee had ever touched her skin, even by accident. They'll touch my dress . . . my hair . . . but they won't touch me, she drummed in her head, groping for a plan.

But anyone could launch an arrow through her back without touching her, and tonight every man carried his bow.

Slowly, she walked through the blinding smoke for the third time. Now she stood at the brink: only one more pass to make through the smoke. The priest grimaced at her through the haze, his face illuminated only where the wetness of his tears reflected the red gleam from the coals. The people's sobbing and wailing threatened to smother her. "Not for long does she lift her foot, not for long does she set out walking," they sang.

She choked through the smoke. Her hands were tied. She had no horse. She had no weapon. Yet a feeling of invulnerability flooded her. She would not die. She had fought too hard for too long to die now. Intermingled with the crying voices a faraway song seeped into her, long neglected and almost forgotten. It hummed faintly at first, but as she recognized and welcomed it, it reverberated in her breast with absolute conviction: I am the Great One!

That instant the Pawnee song ended. The echo of the last word receded slowly into the night among muffled sobs. She absorbed a strange comfort from the thrumming of the rain on the roof, as if she were safe and dry in her own bed.

"Hurry," Wolfstar whispered at her elbow. Her eyes caught a twitch of his hands in the darkness, wanting to shove her toward the smoke.

The girl looked into Wolfstar's face.

She said slowly, "You can't touch me." She turned toward the smoky black, to the many more enemies she could not see surrounding her. "I am the Great One. None of you can touch me." Then resolutely she turned and walked toward the entrance tunnel.

No Pawnee moved or spoke.

Her bound hands outstretched, she hurried through the darkness toward the sound of the rain. She stumbled over someone and slammed her shoulder against a wall, followed the wall with her hands as it opened into the passageway. Her eyes and nose were running so badly from the smoke that for an instant she did not notice the rain streaming down her face.

She was out, but she could see almost nothing through billowing sheets of water in the dark gray of dawn. The stunned gathering behind her began to crawl with confusion. She ran.

Her bound hands swung and bounced crazily off her thighs as the long grass, beaten down by the rain, snatched at her feet like snares. She squinted through the water pouring into her eyes, unable to wipe it away, searching for something, a horse, anything. The calfskin dress and moccasins quickly grew heavy with water, until she was lurching along, every step planting itself by accident. Behind her, shouting voices wove through the rain.

Suddenly her feet slid out from under her. She flipped sideways into the ground, and as her shoulder blade struck she felt the thong between her wrists snap. Pain surged through her shoulder, but her hands were free. She floundered in the soaking dress as if in a spider's web. Clutching the slick grass, she finally pulled herself to her feet. Before she could stand, however, something grasped the scruff of her dress and yanked her upright.

Wolfstar. His eyes blazed with something she had never seen before. Screaming, she struggled to wrench herself from his grasp.

"Down in the wash," he shouted over her cries and the roar of the rain, thrusting his free hand out toward the gully ahead.

"Never!" she shrieked, twisting away from him.

"Bull is down in the wash," he shouted at her as she started to run in the opposite direction.

She stopped.

"Hurry! They're coming!" He flung his arm toward where the earth dropped away a few paces beyond him. "Your horse is waiting in the gulch."

She stood paralyzed. Did he really mean to help her, or was this another pretense to lure her to her death? Her gaze flashed from the ravine's edge to Wolfstar's wildly lit face, and back again. She could hear voices closing behind her.

"Hurry!" Wolfstar screamed.

She hesitated another instant, then bolted for the edge of the gulch and leaped off.

Plunging feet first down the sheer incline, she careened through the crumbling mud, barely able to kick one foot out in front of the other. At the bottom, knee-deep in the floodwater raging through the wash, stood Bull. She slammed into his side.

He began rearing and she grasped at his neck and back to stop him. He wore no saddle, but she managed to grab a saddlebag.

"It's me, Bull, it's me," she cried, struggling to gain her footing in the current. She groped along his face and found the knot that held him to his tether, but her stiff fingers were slimy with grease-paint and rain and mud and she could not loosen the swollen leather. From far above she heard sharp voices. Frantically she dug at the slippery lump.

"Steady," she said in a voice as close to soothing as she could make it, trying to shove the bridle off as Bull snarled, but he wrenched his head away. Her fumbling hands caught the tether. The stake!

She seized the rope and followed it hand over hand into the gray torrent until she felt the stake. She jerked mightily and it sucked out of the mud.

A cry came from above. She looked up and saw through the rain someone standing at the edge of the bluff, silhouetted against the brightening gray sky. His hands were moving as though treading water. Then, slowly, like a great tree, he fell. He toppled headlong down the embankment and crashed into the water twenty paces downstream.

She stomped toward him, clinging to Bull's bridle. Even before she drew close enough to recognize the form thrashing against the current, she knew it was Wolfstar.

The freshly broken shaft of Two-voices' distinctive red arrow jutted from the boy's back.

She loosed one hand from Bull's bridle, snatched the dragging tether, and threw it to Wolfstar. "Tie it around yourself," she shouted.

"Go!" he gasped. "They are fetching horses."

The girl whipped the loose end of the tether around Wolfstar's chest and knotted it. Bull snorted fiercely and pulled back at this weight, but she yanked him forward. She hooked her hand under Wolfstar's arm and heaved him to his feet.

"Climb on," she commanded, crouching to boost him up. With a groan he managed to swing a leg up and catch his heel on Bull's rump, and she threw her weight into shoving him over the top. He sat hunched over like an old woman, bright blood washing through his shirt.

With horror she realized there was nothing in the wash but water and mud. No trees, no ledges, nothing to step up on.

"Help me!" she cried, twisting tight a handful of matted mane and reaching out her free hand.

Wolfstar hesitated, his gaze locked on the bare, black-grease-painted hand streaming with rain.

"Help me!"

He bit his lip and grasped her outstretched hand,

clapped his other hand around her wrist, and with a groan heaved her, belly down, across Bull's withers, like a carcass thrown over a packhorse. Hanging there, she pounded Bull's ribs with everything in her.

"Go!" she shouted. "Go!" And as she twisted around and found her seat, Bull broke into a gallop.

23

WOLFSTAR COULD BARELY HOLD ON TO THE GIRL
and was in such danger of being vaulted off Bull's back
that she reined the animal to a stop in mid-stride, and
turned to secure Wolfstar.

They had been riding hard into the driving rain, in a direction she hoped was toward the sunset, and had
emerged on the other side of the storm. Behind them,
the morning sun appeared as a bright spot in the low-
hanging blanket of cloud. They must have started with a
long enough lead for Bull's stamina to favor them, for
she had seen no sign of their pursuers. Still, the Pawnee
might come charging over the horizon at any moment.
She dared linger only long enough to cinch something
around Wolfstar's ribs to staunch the bleeding, and strap
him onto the horse's back.

But one glance at Wolfstar told her that he could ride
no farther. His skin, glittering with sweat, wore a gray

cast, as if his blood had drained utterly. He was shivering. He sucked at the air but could not seem to find any, for it gurgled out his back around the broken arrow shaft.

Anxiously she scanned the horizon. She saw nothing but yellow hills rolling off to the distant sky.

"Leave me—I'm dying," Wolfstar said in her ear. "Save yourself."

If she escaped, they would hunt her down, he had once said. She urged Bull to the top of a hillock and wheeled him about, peering toward the horizon. The flattened grass was still soaking and the wind gusted cool and damp. In the distance a ragged line of trees showed between hills.

No movement.

She turned Bull back down the hill and slid off his withers. Her face was burning.

"I won't leave you to die," she told Wolfstar sharply, ashamed of having considered the idea.

Her legs were weak and she leaned on Bull as she rummaged hurriedly through a saddlebag.

She did not know what she hoped to find, but the bag, packed with dried buffalo meat and pumpkin rings, did not contain it. She stepped around Bull's head and shoved aside a bow and quiver to dig through the other saddlebag. For the first time she noticed her tightly packed grizzly robe strapped to Bull's hindquarters.

"Here, wrap yourself in this," she said, pulling his knife from its sheath and cutting the robe loose. She draped it over his shoulders, then cut the tether off his waist and eased him from the big horse and onto his side in the grass. To touch him, after so long not touching him, was terrifying and sweet.

"I will return soon," she said, and led Bull up beside a rock outcropping from which she could mount. Landing on his back, she kicked hard, and they raced off in the direction of the trees.

Cheeks stuffed with the inner bark of a cottonwood tree, she chewed hastily as she mounted Bull. But, facing the hills, she abruptly stopped chewing. Fear prickled through her. Which was the hill she had left Wolfstar beside?

She rode ahead, cleaving to the hilltops so she might see farther. If she did not crest the right hill, she might walk past Wolfstar. And the right hill was impossible to distinguish among a thousand of its brothers. She stopped and started, afraid to ride too quickly and pass him by, afraid to slow down for fear she would not reach him in time.

Atop a hill, she turned Bull in a complete circle. In every direction she looked out over hundreds of nearly identical hills. She had lost even the memory of which way the cottonwoods stood.

At the corner of her vision she saw a reddish ridge, but it was lost again in the billowing grass. Uncertainly, she trotted Bull down between the swells, peering ahead.

Then she saw it directly: her grizzly robe.

She kicked Bull forward and slid off him at a run, falling to her knees beside the pelt. She opened and spread it away from Wolfstar. His eyelids were closed tightly. He lay slightly curled in on himself, clutching his medicine bag. Relief flooded through her at the sight of the nearly imperceptible rise and fall of his chest. He was alive, though his breath came shallow and rapid.

She spat a mouthful of pale mush onto the bearskin. "This is the nearest I could find to aspen bark," she said, skinning away his shirt as she talked. "Back home, I have seen a medicine man cure wounds with aspen bark. Even deep wounds; Cut-ear had an arrowhead broken off in his leg, and now he walks without a limp. Have you ever seen an aspen? I am sure this will work," she babbled.

"I thought you had left me," Wolfstar whispered. His body shuddered like leaves in a wind, then was still. For one reeling instant she feared he had died. Her eyes scanned his face. It was twisted as if in a scream, and tears trickled from his clenched eyes.

He was crying not in physical pain, but in the other kind of pain.

"I told you I would not leave you," she said, watching him, grasping at some way to keep him alive. He lay quietly now, wincing.

"Don't you know by now, my grizzly robe is far too important to me to leave behind?" she dared to joke.

The wet crinkles around his eyes deepened, and the

corner of his mouth curved upward. Relieved for no reason, she laughed emptily.

"I must just take this shaft out of you," she said as though she knew what she was doing. She had never pulled an arrow from a live creature. When she hunted, she did not bother with the arrowheads until well into butchering. This one would be difficult to remove, for the bone point protruding from his skin in front was wedged between two ribs. She must force the arrow completely through him.

"As soon as you are well enough to travel, we will head to my country," she said, her mouth dry. A thickish fluid bubbled out around the broken shaft when he breathed.

"You'll see the most amazing places along the way," she continued. "I will show you where the Elk River falls into a golden canyon as high as fifteen or twenty of your earth lodges."

"I never wanted you to die," Wolfstar said quietly.

"I know, I know now."

"You once asked me about Dreamer's name. He dreamed an important dream, I told you. But I did not tell that this dream was about you. Of course, at first we did not know it was about you. The Morning Star has been sending this dream to my people since the beginning of time, demanding the sacrifice of a girl. Understand, we do not want to do it—we must! My people will perish if we do not give the Morning Star his due."

"Don't talk now," she said, shaking. "Here, bite down." She slid the handle of his knife between his jaws. "I will be as quick as I can." In the damp grass she wiped her hands until nothing was left of the grease-paint but gray and rose stains. Then she knelt behind him, wrapped both hands around the arrowshaft, and braced her elbows against her rib cage.

She shoved with all her strength and Wolfstar screamed. The shaft did not move.

"Don't worry," she said, trying to keep her voice even. "I will manage from the front." Gently she rolled him onto his back. Crying out in agony, Wolfstar let the knife fall from his mouth.

She touched the bruised skin where the arrowhead poked through. "I will have to press on your ribs very hard," she said. She began telling him again of the Land of Boiling Waters as she placed her hands on his rib cage. Something cold skimmed her wrist. Wolfstar's hand.

"No," he said in a voice startlingly like his stepfather's. "Just be with me." Laboriously, he shifted to relieve the pressure on the shaft in his back.

Not letting his words into her head, she uselessly mounded her cottonwood-bark poultice around the wound. Though she knew Wolfstar was dying, she talked on of the marvelous places she would show him along their journey, and the people he would meet in her village, and the new life they would lead there.

"Give me your hand," Wolfstar interrupted in a breathy voice. Hesitantly, she took his hand. It was cold and frightening.

"I have not long to live. Let me speak." A tear ran down his cheekbone to his ear.

"All my life," he said, "or all of it that I remember, I have been the young Wolf Star bundle keeper. This is what I *am*." He turned his head and looked into the grass. "Every day of my life I have known: someday the survival of my people will depend on me. When the Morning Star calls again for a sacrifice, it will fall to me to guard the girl. I must be strong inside, clever and kind, so she will do anything I ask; for she must go through the ceremony of her own free will," he whispered, sending a biting chill through her.

"I was prepared!" he gasped angrily. "But how could I know the girl would be you . . ." Tears slipped down the sides of his shaven head.

"When I saw the Spirit Star rise like fire so briefly," he murmured, "I knew that the great person whose death he foretold was you. And I feared we were wrong to take your life. I don't know," he cried. "Are Pawnee dreams more important than Apsaalooka dreams? Are our gods more important than your gods? All I know is I could not bear to deliver you to your death. I could not do it."

His tenderness pierced her heart like a lance.

"I fear . . . my father can never forgive me," he said in a heavy voice.

She smoothed the sweaty strip of hair from his forehead. "He will. Someday he will understand."

They were silent awhile.

"This is the first time I have ever done anything the young Wolf Star bundle keeper was forbidden to do," Wolfstar said. "It feels—like all those places you tell about. It feels like touching a cloud. Thank you for showing me courage." He began coughing, and she sat by helplessly until he caught his breath again. "I hope . . . the Morning Star will be satisfied with my life," he whispered.

The sting in her eyes was overpowering and she could not look at him.

He tried to speak again. She bent low to hear him. "I can't . . . I don't understand," she said.

Slowly, he lifted his left arm and laid it across the other, then pressed his wrists fiercely to his chest.

She clenched her whole face to squeeze back the tears. *I love you, also,* she signed in return.

For some time there was no sound but the breeze across the prairie grass and the gurgling of Wolfstar's punctured back. Then Wolfstar began struggling to sit up, gasping for air. "What will become of me?" he said with sudden strength, as though crying out to the stars. "I have betrayed the stars!"

"The stars will forgive you for following your heart," she said, although she, too, was afraid. "They must. The Spirit Star shone for you, Wolfstar." She worked an arm under his back and slid her other hand under his head and held him. Rocking gently, she began to sing to him in a wavering voice, "Even worms, each other they-them-love."

Wolfstar said nothing more before his spirit-soul left

186

him. The girl kept cradling him and singing, her voice growing hoarse, until, when the sun had climbed high overhead, his body-soul, too, drifted away. The end of her song left a tremendous silence on the vast, windy plain.

She looked down at his lifeless face, and a drop of water splashed on it. Another fell, and another. And suddenly a terrible live thing in her burst from her throat. She heard herself shrieking, and tears began streaming down her face.

It was not true that she had no tears in her. She had cried as a baby, watching the colorful toys they spiraled above her brother's cradleboard, straining for the sounds of their voices. She had cried, but her father poured water down her nose, and it was such a horrible drowning, dying feeling she quickly learned to stop. After that, whenever she began to cry, Chews-the-bear simply said, "I am going to fetch the water," and she would gulp back her tears.

For so long she had frozen every tear before it fell, each time she dreamed of her mother and woke to none, each time the village children had turned away or insulted her as she passed, each time her father greeted her accomplishments with "There is no room in a warrior's heart for vanity." Her tears numbered as many as the stars. And instead of falling, they had grown inside her into a great icy rage.

Now the tears were melting, one by one. They hurt worse than any wound, like the pain when frozen limbs are warmed back to life.

24

THE MOON EASED FROM BEHIND A LONG CLOUD
bank and again revealed the landmarks they had been
riding for through the night: a huge bluff rising from the
flat like a sudden mountain, and to one side, nearer, a
stone needle piercing the sky.

Behind Bull dragged a makeshift travois of cottonwood
saplings, and atop it, wrapped in the grizzly robe, Wolfstar's body. The girl looked straight ahead, seeing nothing,
feeling nothing. She was numb as a stone in winter. She
had been riding all night, and all the day before, stopping
only twice, to pass water.

The moon was setting when she reached the foot of
the bluff. It was higher than it had looked from a distance, and too steep for Bull to attempt. She loosed his
saddlebags and tossed them onto the bear hide alongside
the body. With Wolfstar's knife she cropped off what had
grown back of Bull's mane and tail. She stuffed the hair
into a saddlebag, lashed the robe closed, and secured its

ropes around her body. Without looking up, she began to climb the bluff. It was difficult with Wolfstar's weight dragging behind her. Several times she followed a cut or a slope that looked promising, only to find that farther ahead it grew too steep to continue. All she could do was keep moving.

The sky was beginning to lighten when the girl finally reached the flat top of the bluff and heaved the body after her. Prickles of light swam before her, and she leaned over, hands on her knees, waiting for the light-headedness to pass. Wind whipped across the plateau, heedless of sage and stunted scrub pines. The bluff was so large that a few steps inward one could forget that this was not the prairie itself.

The grave should have a view. She remembered that toward the sunset ran the river she and her captors had followed to this place. Bowing her head against the wind, she set out for that side of the bluff. A number of hares sprang out of her path as she walked, but her eyes did not follow them.

She chose a large outcropping that looked down on the river snaking below and was narrow enough to offer a view of both sunrise and sunset. At that moment the sun was rising bloodred.

"Here you can touch a cloud," she said softly.

The dirt was too dry; the instant she broke into the crust it crumbled to dust and was blasted off the bluff's edge by the wind. She would merely pile rocks on top of the body. It did not matter, for there seemed to be nothing but hares on this barren rock, and they would not meddle with flesh.

She untied and opened the bearskin, half expecting to see again the rapid rise and fall of Wolfstar's chest, but it was as still as she felt inside. His skin was faded, not the rich brown that it had been in life.

She struggled to think ahead, to a future when this would all be a memory.

Wolfstar was gone. She might never cry away her grief for him. But she had earned a place among her people. She would tell the story of her grizzly robe at their fires, and they would sing songs of her, and finally no one could doubt that she was the Great One.

It was not thirst for glory that led her thoughts down this path; she was merely grasping for a reason to go on.

Thus she pushed down her tears as she dragged the body into place near the point of the outcropping and began laying out his things beside him. She gave him most of the dried buffalo meat and pumpkin rings, and he could refill the waterskin from the river below. Bull's mane and tail would give him plenty of horses. She thought of leaving him the bow and quiver, but he was no hunter, so they would be little use to him. She drew his knife from her twisted-hair belt and slid it into the sheath on his breechcloth.

A robe!

Her mouth dried up. The only robe on this vast prairie was her own. Her grizzly hide.

He must have a robe; this was the Moon-when-the-leaves-fall, and bitter cold could come at any moment. There were the buffalo she had seen, but it might take days to bring one down, and time to tan, and she did not know whether the Pawnee were still tracking her. Desperately she argued with herself. She needed a robe, too, after all. But she was good with a bow; she could manage until she found game to make a new robe.

But she needed *this* one.

"Born-great!" she shouted, but even as the name left her mouth she knew it was not his doing. Her rage and grief could only flail at nothing. There was no one to blame for it all, no enemy to fight against.

"I am sorry, Wolfstar," she sobbed. "But—this robe is all I have left." She pulled the robe up to her face and buried her tears in the thick, greasy-smelling hair. "It is all I have left."

Suddenly she thought of the necklace . . . The burnished ivory claws around Wolfstar's throat gleamed enticingly. She could leave him the hide and take the necklace. Surely he would want her to have it. She struggled with herself, watching the blond fur she had cut so precisely to fit between each claw flatten in the harsh wind.

No one would know.

Shame billowed through her. This boy, this boy who was a man, had laid down his life for her!

With great effort she lifted the big, reddish-gold pelt

over Wolfstar's body, over the necklace, and tucked it around him.

She caressed the fur one last time. Then she covered it with stones until it disappeared.

She stood over the grave and cut her arms and legs with a piece of flint, and felt the pain, and it was good to be able to feel. As the blood flowed out of her body, so did the tears. To her shame she was mourning the grizzly robe as well. But she could not help herself.

She was so filled with the other kind of pain she did not think it could ever be washed out of her. "You are gone," she cried, "do not turn back. We wish to fare well."

She stepped to the edge of the bluff and stood a long time, staring out over the prairie below. She felt very small inside.

What did she have to live for now? Everything was gone. She thought of how she had struggled for a place in the world for so long. All she had ever lived for now seemed foolish and far in the past. There was no glory in killing. No glory in glory. Nothing.

She looked down. The bluff was steep as a cliff here, and very high. With one step it would be over.

But Wolfstar had died to save her. If she ended her life, his death, his betrayal of his father, his betrayal of his entire nation—all of these would have been in vain.

Again shame washed through her. What was her suffering—the suffering of one person—in the face of all that had been lost that she might live? She thought not only of what Wolfstar had given, but also of her brother's death. Suddenly she realized the horror of his being trampled by horses, of his life lost so young. This was his fate, to fulfill her path as the Great One. And before him, her mother had died giving them life. She thought of all her father had suffered for her to be the Great One. She thought of the mysterious gift giver from her childhood, and she knew somehow that there had been many— many wise enough to know that she could not have accepted their gifts by light of day.

Wolfstar had been right: her life was not really her own. It belonged to her family, her people . . . and to Wolfstar, and his family and his people—perhaps to all people, perhaps to the universe. She had no right to take her life. No, somehow, somehow, she must try to make her life worth all that had been given for it.

But what in her could possibly be worth such a price? The idea that she was worth saving, worth dying for, seeped into her and filled her with tears. She began to look upon herself with a strange reverence, as a priest looks upon a sacred bundle—something to be treated and wielded with utmost care.

That she was the Great One seemed to mean something different now: a life not of glory, but of duty. A life of struggling to be worthy of the honor.

She began to tremble with the enormity of her task.

She did not know how she would do it, but this new

sense of purpose filled her as nothing had ever filled her before. Perhaps Broken Branch could guide her. He seemed to know there was something valuable in her. She would go back to their valley, to his lodge, and when he came to the doorway, she would tell him, "I am ready."

This time, it would be true.

She looked at Wolfstar's grave for a long time, touching the arrowhead dancing from her ear in the wind. It comforted and strengthened her.

"Your death will not be in vain, Wolfstar," she vowed. "None of it will be in vain."

As she turned away she felt light. Full of light. There was a fire in her, people had said; now it was no longer the raging, insatiable blaze of a bad heart, but a steady, rare, red-gold flame.

And suddenly she knew her name.

Somewhat lightened of her burdens, Grizzlyfire descended the great bluff, mounted her horse, and turned toward home.

AUTHOR'S NOTE

The territory that Grizzlyfire traveled through in this book is now part of Montana, Wyoming, and Nebraska. The great bluff, now Scotts Bluff National Monument in Nebraska, was used in the 1840s and 1850s as a landmark by settlers traveling westward on the Oregon Trail. In 1872, the "Land of Boiling Waters" became the world's first national park: Yellowstone. The obsidian cliff still stands in the park, and is protected by law. However, obsidian—a natural volcanic glass—is quarried from other deposits around the world. Obsidian was prized by Indians throughout North America for its amazing sharpness, and has been used in modern times for some surgical blades, as it can achieve a sharper edge than steel.

Grizzlyfire's people, the Apsaalooka (named after a bird that is long extinct), are better known by the English mistranslation of their name, the "Crow." Many Crow people still live in their historical homeland of southern Montana, on a reservation. Although it was rare for Crow girls to become warriors, it was not forbidden. One female warrior even earned the name Woman Chief. And while it was not a requirement for chiefhood, stopping to rescue a fallen comrade was perhaps the most heroic deed a Crow warrior could perform.

Because the Plains Indians consisted of many different peoples, or tribes, with different languages, they used a widely understood sign language to communicate between tribes. It was also used among people who spoke the same language, when silence was desirable. This language is separate and distinct from the sign language commonly used today by the hearing-impaired.

Different tribes also practiced different religions, although some tribes shared certain general spiritual beliefs, such as a reverence for the number four and a belief in multiple souls. For almost all Plains peoples, medicine men and women (people, sometimes called shamans, who had some special relationship to the spirit world and often performed medical services) and priests (holy people trained in religious rituals) were important to spiritual life.

At the time of this story (the mid-eighteenth century), the Skidi, or "Wolf," band of Pawnee had been performing the Morning Star sacrifice for so many years that no one knows when it began, and the details of why it was performed are no longer clear. Some anthropologists think it may have been adopted between 1506 and 1519 from the Aztec of Central America, who practiced a similar ritual. In 1817, Pitaresaru, the son of a Pawnee chief, rescued a girl from the altar as she was about to be killed. Although the Pawnee had always believed the sacrifice to be a religious necessity, and vital to their survival, they were so deeply affected by this rescue that they ceased the practice. Some Pawnee disagreed with this decision, and two or three sacrifices were rumored to have been performed by the dissenters over the next few years, but the ceremony then died out.

At the time the Morning Star ceremony was abandoned, approximately twelve thousand Pawnee were living in the central Nebraska area in the manner of their ancestors, relatively unaffected by European expansion. According to the 1910 U.S. Census, however, only 610 Pawnee remained. Today the Pawnee people survive, but their traditional way of life, like that of most Native Americans, has been lost forever.

Thanks are due to many people and institutions who helped in the development of this book. For assisting my research, thanks to Yellowstone National Park naturalists David La-Conte, Roy Renkin, and Paul Schullery; Crow Agency Bilingual Materials Development Center director Marlene Walking Bear; and instructor Sharon Stewart-Peregoy and archivist Magdalene Moccasin from Little Bighorn College. For access to their collections, thanks to the libraries at the

University of Michigan and the University of California at Berkeley, the Nebraska State Historical Society, and the New York Public Library. Of course, any errors that the book may contain are solely mine.

For her critique of an early draft, thanks to editor Maureen Sullivan. For encouragement that has never been forgotten, I am grateful to my teachers, especially Viola Diegel, Esther Hiller, Patricia Fingleton, Margaret Rothstein, and Marianne Zubryckyj. For incisive editing, commitment to the project, and sheer stamina, thanks to my editor, Wesley Adams. For moral support and clearheaded perspective throughout the process, thanks to Stephen Fletcher. For a summer of happy plot discussions in the office on Main Street, thanks to my brother Dale. For everything, Emmanuel Schreiber. For financial support that made this book possible, as well as for invaluable encouragement, thanks to my father. And finally, I am thankful to my mother, for prodding me all my life to follow my dream, and for the little glass bear whose task it is to spur me on in her absence.